BLOOD O

By Montiese McKenzie

There are too many people to thank, I will try my best to be brief.

To Mrs. Varella, for encouraging my first story and never realizing those dictionary punishments would give me a lifetime love of words.

To Ashlee, for your help and friendship even when I was a total curmudgeon about it.

To Danielle, for my cover art work and for all the Photoshop ship pics over the years.

To my LiveJournal girls who became the best friends I could ever ask for in life, y'all know who y'all are.

For Shauna and Liz, who listened and loved me no matter what. For Bobby Burke, who helped me understand Alexander in a way I wasn't sure I'd be able to. For my grandmother, who didn't live to see this moment but knew I had what it took to make it happen.

For Roland, the most awesome of nephews, dream big, kid…always.

Table of Contents

CHAPTER 1

The elevator door opened and FBI Special Agent Alexander Rubidoux stepped into the underground garage. It was a warm night, early September in the nation's capital. As he listened to the click-clack of his expensive loafers on the concrete Rube, as he was known to most, felt a chill run through him. He turned and looked behind him. No one was there, the lot was deserted. Rube kept walking, it was late and past time for him to go home.

The hairs on the back of his neck stood up and Rube stopped walking again. He turned around completely; there was nothing there. The agent chuckled to himself. It happened to everyone in the Bureau eventually; paranoia set in. There had been too many cases, too many weirdoes…everyone was a suspect. Even empty parking lots were getting to him. Turning back toward his truck, Rube came face to face with a woman. He let out a sound of surprise and stumbled back.

"The fuck…?" He put his hand on his Glock. You could never be too careful these days.

"Are you Special Agent Alexander Rubidoux?" She asked.

"Who are you?" He gripped the gun tighter.

"Are you Special Agent Alexander Rubidoux?"

"Tell me who you are and maybe we can have a conversation." Rube said.

"My name is Kathryn; I didn't mean to startle you, Agent Rubidoux."

"You could've gotten yourself shot." He let go of the Glock. "You shouldn't sneak up on people in deserted parking lots. Why are you hiding down here?"

Her dark eyes darted back and forth as if she suspected someone had followed her or was listening in the shadows. Rube definitely knew the feeling.

"We can't talk here." She said. "Could you meet me someplace more private?"

"I don't think so. Excuse me; I've had quite a long day."

"Agent Rubidoux!" Kathryn's voice stopped him from walking away. It reverberated through the empty space. "I need your help. Please; it's a matter of life and death."

Rube turned and looked at her. He had been reading people long before the Federal Bureau of Investigation recruited him. He was 6'2" so that made Kathryn, if that was even her name, 5'7" at most. She was wearing high heeled boots that gave her another two to two and a half inches. Her shoulder length hair, black as a raven's, was parted in the middle.

She had flawless dark brown skin, not a scar or blemish in sight. She wore faded blue jeans a, a white tank top, and a black bra with those boots. If she had a weapon on her it would be hard to hide…her clothes clung in all the right places. *As a woman's should*, his father used to always say. Rube hated when he said that.

"Whose life or death?" He asked.

"Someone I care for very much, and possibly my own."

He continued to look at her. Rube had been lied to more times than he could count. Both good liars and bad took their cracks at him. Kathryn was either an excellent liar, on the level of sociopaths, or she was telling most of the truth. Sighing, he decided to take a chance.

"What kind of danger are you in? To meet a stranger somewhere I'm going to need a little more than life and death."

"My husband has been kidnapped." Kathryn spoke in a low voice.

"Have you contacted the police?"

"Please Agent Rubidoux; I don't have a lot of time."

"Where can I meet you?" Rube asked sighing. It had been a long day. It looked as if it would be a long evening as well.

"There's a little coffee shop called Cups on 16th, off of Potomac. Meet me there in twenty minutes."

"If this is a trick…"

"Just meet me there. Please."

She turned and was gone as fast as she'd shown up. Rube looked all around the garage but saw no trace of her. He didn't like this but something told him to drive to the coffee shop anyway. Rube hadn't gotten this far in life from ignoring his gut. Still, he wasn't going to drive his personal vehicle to a situation he knew nothing about.

Bypassing his Chevy Silverado, Rube took a set of keys out of his pocket and walked over to one of the FBI issued SUVs. He climbed in, started the ignition, and headed to a coffee shop he didn't even know existed. It was only Wednesday; this week did not need to go any further downhill.

***

The place was small, a little off the beaten path, and didn't look like it seated more than 30 people. There were some cozy couches, where a couple sat and whispered to one another. A teenage girl, if Rube wasn't mistaken Goth was her style, sat in the corner with an iPod and a laptop. The woman he knew as Kathryn sat at a small table near the window. She held a large coffee cup in her hand and looked nervous. She also looked frightened. When she saw him, she called him over with her eyes. Rube sat across from her in a comfortable plush chair.

"I never knew this place existed." He said. "It's nice."

"It's a specialty place." Kathryn replied. "Everything is made to your liking."

When the server came over, Rube ordered a hot blackberry and pomegranate tea with a blackberry scone.

"What happened to your husband?" He asked.

"He was taken."

"By whom? Were you told not to contact the police? Was a ransom demand made?"

"Have you ever heard of Operation: Eternity, Agent Rubidoux?" Kathryn asked.

"No." he shook his head.

"Your federal government is trying to find the key to eternal health and life." Kathryn replied.

"That's my tax dollars hard at work." Rube mumbled.

"They want to use my husband to do it. He has friends in high places, for all I know he was helping them at one point. But he did not disappear voluntarily."

"Is he a scientist?"

"No."

"Kathryn, I need you to answer my questions or I'm leaving." Rube said, clearly exasperated. His tone returned to neutral when he thanked the server for the tea and scone. "In the time you spend beating around the bush and being vague your husband could be dying."

"Do you know Paul Kirsch?" She asked.

"If you're speaking about the international financier; I know of him. Why?"

"He's my husband. Well, not my husband but we've been together quite a long time."

Rube had no idea that Paul Kirsch was in an interracial relationship, not that he spent much time thinking about or reading up on the man. But he watched him on C-Span or MSNBC when he couldn't sleep at night. That was more often than Rube liked. A year or so back he heard that Kirsch was in the running to be Chairman of the Federal Reserve but it never came to pass. He was still the go-to money man when it came to a lot of government spending and finance.

"Agent Rubidoux, Paul Kirsch is a vampire and so am I."

"I'm sorry?" the teacup was halfway to his lips. He put it down on the table and looked at her. Rube had no idea what his face looked like but he could make an educated guess. Kathryn's was serious, not an ounce of jest.

"I said…"

"I heard you and I don't have time for these kinds of games." Rube pushed his chair back and stood. "You dragged me down here for this?"

"Please sit down."

"This is…"

"Sit down, Agent Rubidoux." Kathryn's brown eyes turned completely black like demons in the movies. Her voice went deep, sharp fangs slid out of her gums, and her nails grew long.

"Jesus Christ…" Rube flinched, the words barely coming out of his constricted throat.

"If you sit down I will do my best to explain." Kathryn said, closing her eyes. When she opened them again they were normal. The nails and fangs were also gone.

"I really don't think I want to know." Rube sat back in the chair. His stomach was in his shoes and he had to work very hard not to vomit. What in the hell was happening? Was someone playing a trick on him? If he had more friends that might have been something to consider. "You're telling me that vampires really exist. You're telling me that you're one of them."

"Lots of things that you don't even think about exist, agent. The government kidnapped Paul because they want to do experiments on him to see if he holds the key to eternal human life."

"How do you know this?"

"I have my sources." Kathryn said.

"Forgive me, but your sources sound a little farfetched."

"I need to get Paul back and to do that I need your help. I don't care what you believe or don't believe, I just know you're the best."

"Did you hear that from your sources as well?" Rube asked.

"No one knows that we're talking and it needs to stay that way." She replied. "I researched you after I read an article in the *Washington Post*. You saved that bank executive's daughter from a serial kidnapper. You're just who I need."

"When did Paul go missing?" If this was for real, Rube intended to treat it like a normal kidnapping. The kooky questions would surely come later.

"At approximately 10:45 this morning. He never made it to his meeting at the OEOB."

"It hasn't even been 24 hours; he might not be gone at all. You think the government took him?"

Kathryn didn't think it, she knew. Her source was as reliable as one could be, even if the information was spotty at best. Vampires had been disappearing for years, here and there. The numbers weren't high enough to be considered epidemic but everyone in her world knew about it. They were just gone without a trace; never heard from again.

This morning Kathryn's life was as normal and boring as always. Now she was in a nightmare she could not wake up from. She was already awake…this was real. The lore used to keep their children in line just hit home like a ton of bricks.

"I think you should report him missing." Rube said, not believing most of what he just heard. He knew what he saw and the image quickly burnt itself into his subconscious but what he heard was ridiculous. He'd stepped out of the Hoover Building elevator and into the Twilight Zone. "It could tip the kidnapper's hand. They want their experiments to be a big secret…you can expose them."

"I don't think you realize what you're asking me to do." Kathryn said. "I would be exposing much more than that. It's a risk I will not take."

"Grabbing a famous, international financier was quite gutsy of them." Rube replied.

Kathryn looked at him. She looked at him deeply; could see the skepticism all over him. He probably thought she was mentally ill and didn't know Paul Kirsch from Paul Reubens. She was going to have to put this in terms he understood. Kathryn took a deep breath.

"You probably think I'm a crackpot who's wasting your time, Agent Rubidoux. I can't make you believe everything I've told you; it's a little unbelievable. But this is the truth…no one can know Paul is missing and I must get him back quickly. The lives of our children are at stake."

Her words made him pause. Children were involved in this? Vampires could have children? *Oh stop*, Rube scolded himself, *this woman is not a damn vampire. I don't know what the hell she just did with her eyes and her teeth but she is not a vampire.*

"How many children do you have?" He asked.

"We have two daughters and a son. There's also Charlie, he's family and we're all in danger. There are those who would use our time of weakness to exact revenge on Paul. Whether their reasons are real or perceived, revenge only comes one way in my world…slaughter."

"Slaughter." The word was hard for Rube to spit out. He wasn't going to have the slaughter of a family on his conscience. He'd seen it enough in his business and the pictures kept him up at night.

"The longer Paul is gone, the more difficult it will be to keep the secret under wraps." She said. "I need to get him back and I wouldn't be asking you if I wasn't desperate. If that means exposing myself and my world to a stranger, so be it. I have nothing to lose anymore."

They were both quiet for a while. Kathryn knew he needed some time to let it sink in. She had dug up everything she could find on Alexander Rubidoux. She knew the story she told would be a hard pill to swallow. Kathryn was doing what she had to do to keep her children safe.

"If I take this case, I need to know everything Kathryn. I need to know every bad deal, every friend, enemy, mistress, and disgruntled former employee. I need to know who hates you, what drugs your kids use, all of it. If you lie to me, I will walk. Honesty is the only way we do this. Be honest with me and I might be able to find your husband."

"I already told you what happened to him." Kathryn replied. "And yes, I know it's far-fetched. That doesn't make it a lie."

"You need to give me 48 hours to do this my way." Rube said. "Then I'll look into other options. Now tell me about your life with Paul."

Kathryn finished whatever was in her cup and looked around. More people had come in but calling it crowded would have been off base. Still, it was too crowded for Kathryn's liking. She had taken enough chances tonight. In her world every wall had eyes and ears.

"This is a safe place, Agent Rubidoux, but I can't expose personal business out in the open. The only place I'll ever feel safe doing that is my home."

"Fine," Rube nodded. "Then we'll go there if that's alright with you."

Kathryn flagged the server for the check but was told it was on the house.

"Tell Austin I really appreciate it." She said.

The server nodded and walked away. Kathryn left a $10 bill on the table before she and Rube left.

"Did you drive here?" He asked. "I can follow you."

"I took a cab. I'll have to ride with you."

"I'm parked down here."

The ride to her home was uneventful. Oldies played on the radio and the music relaxed Rube a bit. Kathryn was good at giving directions and soon he was at the American Park estate. He didn't realize manor homes like this still existed in this part of the nation's capital. He pulled up the driveway and they both got out of the car.

They walked up the steps to a long, wraparound porch. Kathryn took keys from her pocket and Rube followed her into a large foyer. He hadn't seen much yet but it was beautiful. Not ostentatious by any stretch, what he could see of the living room was clean and tastefully decorated. Then he looked up and saw a curly haired teenage white boy at the top of the long staircase. He wasn't expecting that. The boy was just staring at them. There was something off-putting about his stare.

"Hey," Kathryn smiled a bit. "Nath…"

She couldn't get his whole name out of her mouth before he flew down the stairs. He didn't literally fly, thank God, but Rube had never seen anyone move so fast. Bearing large, white fangs, his eyes turned black as he hissed and growled low in his throat. He nearly jumped on top of Rube. The FBI agent stumbled back and hit his head on the wall.

"Nathan!" Kathryn shouted. She grabbed him by the scruff of his neck like a mama wolf would a disobedient pup, yanking him out of Rube's face. "What's the matter with you?"

"Who is this?" His voice was deep and dark as Kathryn's had been in the coffee shop when she told Rube to sit down.

"Nathan? Nathan Anton Kirsch," She took hold of his face with her thumb and forefinger. "Nath, look at me love, look at Mother. Calm yourself. Just breathe."

"Why did you bring him into our house?" his fangs retracted into his gums but he was by no means calm.

"Agent Rubidoux is going to help me find your father, though he might change his mind because of your behavior. Apologize this instant."

"I'm sorry, Mother." Nathan's eyes, now bluish green, were downcast. He whispered the apology.

"To him," Kathryn replied firmly. She pointed at Rube, who still stood against the wall stunned.

"I'm sorry." The young man mumbled, not even looking at the FBI agent.

"I'll live." Rube replied, rubbing the back of his head and grateful he wasn't bleeding. He didn't wake up this morning thinking anything like this would happen to him. He'd been on the receiving end of a fair share of attacks in his time but wanted to pat himself on the back for not screaming like a prepubescent girl when faced with young Nathan. What the hell had he gotten himself into?

"Where are your sisters?" Kathryn asked, quickly turning her eyes from Rube to Nathan. She still held onto him.

Rube held onto his Glock. A bullet might not kill a vampire but it could possibly stun him enough for Rube to get the hell out of dodge.

"Johanna's asleep." Nathan replied. "She wanted Father to read her story tonight but I told her that he had to leave town on an emergency work trip. She said he never leaves without saying goodbye to her. I told her that he had to this time but he would return with presents. I don't know if she believed me. I don't like being dishonest with her, Mother."

"I know, my love." Kathryn kissed his temple.

"She can feel it...she knows when I lie."

"I'm going to talk to her tomorrow. Where's Halle?"

"She left." Nathan said.

"What! I told all of you to stay in the house. Where did she go?"

"I don't know. She said she wanted to find out if there was word on the street about Father."

"Jesus," Kathryn ran her hands over her face. "She'll get us all killed. The petulance of that child…she would have never disobeyed her father like this."

"Charlie followed to keep an eye on her. I wanted to stop her but I didn't want to fight with her again."

"Alright, Nath. I'm going to talk to Agent Rubidoux in the library. You go upstairs and try to relax."

She finally let him go and he walked up the stairs much slower than he came down. Kathryn turned to Rube.

"I'm so sorry. Nathan is very close to his father and he's worried. Sometimes he lashes out but he would never harm anyone on purpose."

"He's a vampire." Rube said. He still had a voice; ten points for him.

"We all are, Agent Rubidoux. I told you."

"Johanna…"

"My little one, yes she is as well. Come to the library and we'll talk."

"How old is Johanna?" Rube asked, following her through the living room and down a hallway. Should he ask why Nathan was white, would that be considered rude? Perhaps he was adopted. It was surely none of his business. Whatever the family dynamic, it was clear that to Nathan, Kathryn was his mother. From experience their interaction had beloved mother and son written all over it.

"Do you want to know how old she is or how old she will look to you?" Kathryn asked, waving him toward a chair. "Should I get you some ice for your head?"

"I'm fine." Rube looked around the room, his eyes falling on a painting of the family over the fireplace. They looked like the picture perfect modern American family. Paintings were old school but vampires had no reflection so photographs were probably difficult. He almost laughed, couldn't believe he was going to let himself think that these people might be vampires. There had to be another explanation. "How old will Johanna look to me?"

"Approximately eight." Kathryn sat on the couch and crossed her legs.

"Eight years old? You murdered a child?"

"I haven't murdered anyone, Agent Rubidoux."

"If she is undead then she had to be dead first. Am I right?"

"I would really appreciate if you didn't judge my family. No matter what you think of the choices made concerning my children, the life they live here with their father and I is better than anything they would've had out there alone. I will not justify myself to you…ever. That's surely not why I invited you here."

"Tell me what happened to Johanna. I don't want to judge you; I want to understand. You're telling me that you're vampires, Kathryn. I'm a bit out of my element."

Kathryn felt that was just another form of justification, and she didn't like it. Still, she knew if he was going to help them, Alexander Rubidoux would have to know what he was walking into. He would have to open his eyes wide and expand his mind. She didn't feel as if there was much time but Kathryn would give him a crash course tonight. If he chose to walk away, something in her knew he'd never tell her secrets. They were too unbelievable anyway.

"We were living in Vienna…"

"When?" He asked.

"1938. We were living in Vienna and Halle, our oldest, worked in a hospital. Johanna's family was killed in a car crash and she was barely clinging to life. This was before the days of sophisticated medical technology. She was half-Austrian and half-black, French most likely; she would never receive the kind of care that so-called pure Austrians did. It was a wonder she even made it to the hospital and was kept alive. Halle used to read to her and after a few days she called her father and told him that she wanted to bring the child over. She thought it was the best thing to do."

"What does that mean?" Rube asked.

"It means turning a human into a vampire. Paul forbade her to do it. It's a very serious undertaking and the bond it creates is strong. Halle is impetuous; Paul didn't think she was ready for the responsibility of a child. He also didn't think she had the strength to do what needed to be done properly. He came to me and asked if I wanted a child. Of course I did. So he brought me Johanna."

"She could've passed away peacefully…reunited with her family on the other side." Rube reasoned.

"I think you need to leave." Kathryn stood up. "I don't know what I was thinking to even consider asking for your help. You choose to make judgments about things that happened before you were born instead of focusing on a man who has been snatched in broad daylight. I'm sorry to have wasted your time, Agent Rubidoux. I'm sorry that you wasted mine."

Rube stood too. He was going to say something, not quite sure what, but his thoughts were interrupted by the sound of two approaching voices. It was a young man and woman. Kathryn walked around the couch, meeting them close to the doorway.

"Halle, where the hell have you been?" She demanded.

"Mother!" The young woman was startled. "I didn't know you were back yet."

"Clearly; and what are you wearing? You've been in my closet again."

"You always told me that a woman needs considerable bait to capture big sharks."

"What did you do?" Kathryn asked.

"I didn't do anything. I went out to see if anyone was whispering and gossiping about Daddy's disappearance. You told me not to tell anyone and I didn't."

"I also told you to stay in the house but you deliberately disobeyed me."

"I don't like feeling helpless." Halle replied through clenched teeth from which fangs emerged. "I want to help find Daddy too."

"I know you do, sweetheart." Kathryn caressed her face. "We just have to be careful. This situation is a tinderbox and our emotions can be felt by those around us. I need you to stay inside until I get control of this. Promise me."

"Are you going to find Daddy?" Halle asked.

"I'm doing everything in my power. Now, promise me."

"I promise."

"Uncross your fingers…that's a ridiculous superstition and you know it."

Halle sighed, doing as her mother told her. Kathryn kissed her forehead and hugged her close. She reached out a hand to caress Charlie's face as well. Halle looked at Rube.

"Who's this?" She asked.

"Agent Rubidoux from the FBI," Kathryn replied. "He was just leaving."

"You're in the FBI?" She rushed toward him, though in a quite different manner than her brother had earlier. She and Nathan weren't only polar opposites in their approach to strangers. He was pale white, almost pasty in appearance. Halle's skin was very light; they might call her high yellow where Rube came from. He was never fond of the term. It had been used on his mother more than once…there were always whispers she was "passing".

Her eyes were dark green, determined and focused. Her brother looked weary, almost sickly in his appearance but Halle Kirsch seemed very much full of life. Rube felt uncomfortable looking at her curvy body in a blood red dress that left very little to the imagination. He felt dizzy thinking of her mother in it. "Where is my father?" She demanded. "Where is he, dammit? I know he had some kind of business with you."

"I don't know your father." He said. "I don't know where he is."

"You're one of them though…one of those shady people he sometimes worked with. We will kill every single one of you if he doesn't return safely to us."

"I'm not." Rube shook his head.

"Halle, stop. Your anger at him is uncalled for and helps nothing." Kathryn put her hands on Halle's shoulders. "Agent Rubidoux has nothing to do with your father's disappearance. You need to go upstairs, get out of my dress, and take a relaxing bath. Now, love."

Halle nodded. She turned, kissed her mother's cheek, and left the room.

"Charlie, would you please see the agent out."

"Of course,"

"I'd like to stay." Rube said. "I came here to get information so I can work this case. I'm sorry if I overstepped my bounds. It won't happen again, I assure you."

Kathryn looked at Charlie, who was looking back at her. When she woke this morning, she expected another day in a predictable life that she'd grown rather disgusted with. Nothing could be further from the truth. For almost seventy years, Kathryn had been complacent in letting Paul run the day to day affairs of their lives. She'd gone from educated Russian aristocracy with a thirst for knowledge and a fiery strength to even less than a housewife. She was in an often hostile world that thought of her and her children as less than human because of the color of their skin. It enraged her that over 500 years later she was still fighting the same battle.

There were those who would be content with the life she seemed to have…Kathryn was not. This was not how she wanted to once again come into her own but fear burned off hours ago. She was in survival mode now and after watching the world change around her for half a millennia, Kathryn knew she could do this. She had no other choice in the matter. Living in practical exile didn't leave her with many friends or people she could trust.

Alexander Rubidoux was her best chance of being successful. They didn't have to like each other to work together, that was something Kathryn knew for sure after centuries with Paul. The faster they cut through the bullshit; the faster they got down to business. It was time to get down to business.

"I'm going to tell you what you think you need to know to help me, Agent Rubidoux. Save your judgments for your own time. We don't have to like each other to work together. Just be respectful of me and my family and we'll extend you the same courtesy for as long as you're with us."

"Yes, of course." Rube nodded.

"Alright Charlie, I need to speak with Agent Rubidoux alone. Will you check on the children please?"

"Sure. I'm Charlie Demery, by the way."

"Oh hell, forgive my bad manners." Kathryn said.

"Alexander Rubidoux," Rube extended his hand but the young man just waved. He pulled his hand back. It was the nicest introduction he'd gotten all night so he surely wouldn't complain.

"Are you really going to help us find Paul?" Charlie asked.

"I'll do my best. Your mother…"

"Charlie isn't my son, Agent Rubidoux. He's blood of my blood; family. He and Paul are companions."

"I take care of him and was supposed to be with him this morning." Charlie said, looking down at his at his dusty brown oxfords. A blond lock fell over his eye.

"I'm grateful you weren't." Kathryn replied, once again stroking his face. "Then you would both be gone or even worse, you might be dead. We'll talk in a little while, Charlie."

"Alright." He left the room, sliding the heavy wooden doors closed behind him.

Rube and Kathryn returned to their seats; Kathryn took a deep breath. She told the stranger everything she thought he needed to know to help them. Then she walked him to the door.

"Give me 48 hours on my end to see what I can piece together." Rube said. "We'll meet again on Friday."

"That's a long time. I already told you what happened to him. We don't need to waste precious time."

"Forgive me but your story is a little far-fetched. It could be true but you have to give me some time to find out. Your husband is quite a visible man…his being missing will not go unnoticed."

"That's what I'm afraid of." Kathryn replied.

"How can I get in touch with you?" Rube asked.

"Give me your cell phone."

He didn't know why but he did so without hesitation. Rube watched her quickly type in letters and numbers before handing it back.

"Ekaterina?" He raised an eyebrow.

"That's who I was many years ago. If you're ever separated from that phone, no one will know of our connection."

"Do you have a last name, Ekaterina?"

"I'll tell you when we meet again. Goodnight, Agent Rubidoux."

"You can call me Rube." He said.

"I will not. Do you know what that word actually means?"

"That's what everyone calls me; it's just short for Rubidoux. Alex or Alexander would also be fine but I'm used to Rube. It's not a deal breaker or anything."

"Goodnight, Alexander."

She opened the door for him and watched him walk away. Kathryn knew she blew his mind tonight but also that he'd be back when he said he would. Perhaps his mind wasn't as narrow as some of his brethren. That was something Kathryn would find out soon enough. That would be the difference between life and death.

CHAPTER 2

Rube watched the misty drizzle form on the windshield of his SUV. He was sitting outside of the Kirsch home on Friday evening but hadn't gone in yet. His 48 hours of investigation yielded very little. Paul Kirsch was quite wealthy. He was also enigmatic, according to the paperwork anyway.

There didn't seem to be anyone who knew anything about him really. He wasn't on the FBI's radar, or the SEC's; the dossier Rube managed to cobble together was scarce. According to those in the know, he was actually Paul Kirsch, Jr. His father had emigrated from Eastern Europe after the war and had been in the same business as he was. The Kirschs were a post WWII success story.

Even less information was available on Paul's family. They all existed, had social security numbers and birth certificates, but there was little else. It wasn't easy to hide from the government, especially working in finance and living in a manor. The only way it seemed probable was if the government was helping you live in the shadows. Operation: Eternity kept going through Rube's mind.

That had to be total bullshit. There didn't seem to be another explanation but he wasn't ready to accept that just yet. The government snatching people and harboring secrets was not new or rare. Rube just wasn't sure how deep he wanted to get involved in something like that. If he did, he was going to have to stay far under the radar. A tapping on the driver's side window startled him. He rolled it down, gasping when he saw Kathryn.

"What happened to your face?" he asked.

"It's nothing. I need you to take me somewhere."

"Where? Get in the car."

Kathryn quickly walked around the back of the SUV and climbed into the passenger seat. Rube looked closer at the three gashes on her cheek.

"Kathryn, what the hell happened to your face? Should I take you to an ER?"

"I'll be fine. Nathan got upset...he lashed out." She replied. "He didn't mean to."

"Your son did that to you?" It was impossible to hide his shock. Rube was ready to grab his Taser and give the young man a smack down he would never forget. Fangs, claws, or whatever, the FBI agent's anger was ready to boil over. Alexander Rubidoux was quite a force when he was angry.

"My family is under immense strain, Agent Rubidoux. Nathan is very close to his father and sometimes has difficulty controlling his emotions. He would never hurt me on purpose."

"Don't make excuses for his unacceptable behavior." Rube said. He pointed at her face. "That looks like he hurt you."

"You don't know my son." Her tone was firm. "Anyway, I'm going to be fine."

"Then tell me why he lashed out at you."

Kathryn took a deep breath, running her fingers through her straight raven hair. She was tired of his questions that had little to do with the matter at hand. Rube watched in amazement as the gashes on her face slowly closed up before disappearing altogether. Without his consent, or hers for that matter, Rube's fingers traced the once again flawless black skin. He was surprised that it was warm to the touch. He was surprised, and grateful, she didn't bite him.

"I'm worried about my family's safety. The longer Paul is gone, the more vulnerable we are. I don't have time to constantly watch over the children and work on getting Paul back. Leaving them alone for too long scares me to death. I have a friend who could take them in…somewhere they would be safe."

"A friend like you?" Rube asked.

"She's not a vampire but she is of my world. She would protect them; I trust her with the information that Paul is gone."

"So what caused Nathan to lash out at you?"

"He's terrified, Alexander. He doesn't want to leave me; he already fears that his father could be dead. He didn't mean to hurt me…he's just upset."

"Are you going to send them away?" Rube asked. He would never admit it to her but those kids kinda scared the hell out of him. He'd seen Kathryn's other face and it was nothing to scoff at but her offspring seemed petulant and violent. That wasn't unusual with young adults but they weren't exactly normal young adults, were they?

"They won't go." Kathryn sighed. "My children are stubborn as hell. I still haven't told Johanna the truth about her father's absence. I won't because she'll be petrified. It's bad enough she can feel my tension.

"Halle is ready to come out of her skin because she wants so badly to lead the charge on getting her father home. She's constantly fighting with Charlie and Nathan…there are goddamn claw marks everywhere. Paul is going to be livid when he returns. He hates when the children fight. They actually fight all the time, but never like this. Start the car; we have to go."

"Where are we going?" Rube did as she asked.

"I think I know someone who can help us. Do you need directions to Georgetown?"

"No. I'll get us where we need to be."

***

Rube had never heard of Absinthe but that didn't surprise him. In the past 48 hours it felt as if his skull had been cracked open. All kinds of new information was filtering in but Rube wasn't sure what he would do with it. He followed Kathryn into the bar and looked around the place. It was cavernous and rather dim. Everything was decorated in cherry oaks, maroon, and black lacquer…very tastefully done.

Depeche Mode played over speakers but not so loud that Rube couldn't hear himself think. The crowd looked relaxed; there was drinking, dancing, and lots of conversation. The FBI agent didn't know if he was completely surrounded by monsters. Everyone looked normal. Kathryn approached the bar where an older man made drinks and chatted with patrons.

"Hey," Kathryn said to him. "Is he here, Max?"

"He's at his usual table. What can I get for you, beautiful?"

"A glass of your best."

"And you, friend?" He looked at Rube.

"I'll have whatever lager you have on tap."

"Not a problem."

The guy, apparently named Max, nodded. Kathryn turned to look out at the crowd. She caught sight of him eating and drinking at his table. His constant companion, a large Rottweiler, was with him tonight as well.

"There he is." She said in a low voice.

"Who?" Rube tried to follow her eyes.

"Someone who might help," Kathryn took the goblet of blood Max offered. "C'mon."

Nodding, Rube grabbed his beer and followed Kathryn into the thick of the crowd. They made their way over to the table; Kathryn put her goblet down. The black man, dressed head to toe in black, looked at her and so did the dog. The dog wasn't the one who sighed.

"Well this cannot be good." He grumbled, cutting and tasting his steak.

"I need your help." Kathryn replied.

"Money talks and bullshit walks, your highness. I got bills to pay."

"You owe me, Dev." Kathryn slipped into the booth.

Rube remained standing, eyes scanning the crowd. He wasn't sure what he would do if all hell broke loose but contingency plans were forming in his brain. He'd already scoped out all the exits…at least the place was up to code.

"I owe you nothing, woman. Absolutely nothing. I'm doing the calculations in my head and the total is zero."

"Oh really? So Petrograd is just forgotten? As old as you are Dev, I thought you'd have a better memory."

"How long do you think you're going to be able to use something that happened almost a century ago against me?" Devrim Hisham asked. This conversation was already boring him. He didn't want his costly meal getting cold.

"You killed Natalya." Kathryn said simply.

"That was justified and you know it. She made the decision to go rogue; she paid for it with her life. Paul Kirsch and I have no vendetta."

"That's right, he showed you benevolence and when the shit hit the fan he got you out. Now he needs your help."

"Why'd he send you?" Dev asked, sampling his baked potato and adding pepper. "And what's with the stiff?"

Rube ignored his insult and so did Kathryn.

"What do you know about Operation: Eternity?" She asked.

"Only whispers on the street. I'm sure it exists; that kinda shit is right up the government's alley. Blood suckers have been disappearing without a trace all over the country for at least 20 years, some estimates say 40."

"Well this time they hit pay dirt. They've taken Paul."

"Are you sure?" Dev looked at her. That wasn't pay dirt; that was asking for the wrath of God. He knew Kirsch was into some shady shit, show him a finance guy who wasn't. He also knew he had friends in many branches of the government. Looked like someone was biting the hand that fed them.

"Yes."

"What do you want from me?"

"I want you to keep your ear to the ground around here. I'm working on trying to get him back but I can't do everything on my own. I need to know if it gets out that he's missing."

"He does the Sunday shows damn near weekly. You think people won't notice."

"Believe me, I'm worried that they will."

"Is there someone after you?" Dev asked.

"There's a chance that Michael Marin and his clan might see an opportunity they need to take advantage of." Kathryn replied.

"Fuckin savages," He muttered. "What's that about?"

"Paul killed Julian Black." Kathryn lowered her voice practically to a whisper. "He didn't want to but Charlie's life was in mortal danger. They declared a blood feud…a life for a life. Reapers don't play fair, Dev, you know that. They will slaughter my whole family and I cannot let that happen."

Dev wanted to know what the suit was for. The look on his face when he eyeballed Rube couldn't exactly be called disdain but it came pretty close. Rube held up to the scrutiny.

"Agent Rubidoux's with the FBI; he's helping me on the government end. He'll be able to get into doors that you and I never could. Are you going to help me?"

Dev thought about it as he finished his meat and potatoes. He took his time, finished his beer, and flagged a barmaid for another.

"If I do this, Petrograd is a thing of the past. The next time you want something from me you have to pay for it like everyone else. I don't want it getting around that I'm working pro bono, especially for vampires. I'm not your goddamn errand boy."

"Fine, but…"

"Oh now what?" He didn't bother to hide his exasperation. The Rottweiler growled a bit; Dev petted the dog's gigantic head. "What more could you possibly want?"

"You help me on this, and give me an amulet…then Petrograd is forgotten."

"Give you an amulet?' he laughed a bit. "You must have fallen and bumped your head, sweetheart. That's never happening."

"I need it for Alexander's protection." Kathryn reasoned. "We don't know everything we're up against, Dev."

Dev once again looked Rube up and down. He looked a little too FBI, like he played an agent on TV. The black suit, black spiffy shoes, mediocre tie, and the nearly silver close cropped hair was a walking cliché. Dev was waiting for someone to yell action.

"Forget it."

"Devrim…"

"Look, you know if this gets into the wrong hands, the consequences are immeasurable. I don't have many left and there are those who would kill for one. How can I even trust you'll give it back to me? Bloodsuckers haven't proven themselves that trustworthy over the centuries. This could all be a ruse to get one from me."

"I wouldn't do that. What the hell would I need it for, I'm going to be around forever."

"Spare me the Mary, virgin mother of Jesus routine." He replied, sipping the new beer in front of him. "And I don't even know this guy…I trust humans less than I trust vampires. How do I know he won't be seduced by its power?"

"I plan on letting absolutely none of this, whatever it is, seduce me." Rube replied. "Believe me."

"It's the amulet or Petrograd forever." Kathryn said.

"Dammit, I really don't like you." Dev sighed. He pulled the necklace out of the inside pocket of his black trench coat. He slapped it into Kathryn's open palm. "I'm telling you this; if I don't get it back when this is over…I'm cutting your bastard son's head off."

"That's not funny, Dev. Why would you say something like that?"

"Do I look like I'm joking? I owe that kid an ass whooping anyway."

"Nathan has troubles; you know that." Kathryn replied. "He's never hurt anyone on purpose."

"Troubles?" Dev smirked. "I've followed his troubles through at least ten countries. Don't you get tired of constantly cleaning up after him?"

"Shut up, Dev." She tried to check her tone but her anger was evident.

"I don't understand why Paul doesn't put the world out of its misery and just cut the kid's head off. He's sensible about most things these days except that demon."

"You shut the hell up!" Kathryn exploded. Her eyes went black, her fangs came out, and she grabbed Dev's tee shirt.

The Rottweiler growled loudly but Dev took gentle hold of his dog collar so he wouldn't attack. He was not impressed with Kathryn's game face. Rube looked around to see if anyone noticed the scene but no one was paying attention. For all he knew, this kind of thing was a nightly occurrence around here. If this was Dev's normal attitude then Rube had little doubt.

"Get off my goddamn shirt, Kathryn. Now."

Kathryn sighed and let go. Taking a couple of deep breaths, her face and countenance went back to normal.

"I'm sorry." She said.

Dev shrugged it off. He let the dog go, petted him, and went on with drinking his beer.

"Morian could've ripped your throat out." He said. "Control your temper. We're even, Spencer." He watched her get up and walk away with the FBI agent. "Hey, a word of advice, Jack Ryan, you'll get a little further around here if you ditch the suit. People don't like cops."

"Thanks." Rube held up his hand to wave. He and Kathryn walked out the door. "What is that?"

"Put it on, Alex, and never take it off." She handed him the amulet, silver and amethyst pendant on a silver chain. "It will protect you and that's all you need to know."

"I'm going to need to know more than that." Rube struggled a bit with the clasp but finally got it on. It looked like a harmless necklace but after all he'd seen he wasn't just going to take anyone's word for it. He could be wearing a curse around his neck.

"It gives you immortality." She spoke in a low tone. "Dev is part of a secret group of immortals who protect the few left on earth. Many were stolen or destroyed during the Great War. It doesn't give you complete immortality, you can still be decapitated, but other than that, you're safe. Don't take it off until this is over. Happy now?"

He was certainly not happy. In fact, Rube was sure he would start having decapitation dreams in the very near future. This must have been what David Warner felt like after he saw all those pictures in *The Omen*. There wasn't a damn thing he could do when his time came.

Outside in the cool, drizzly spring night, Kathryn leaned on the brick building. She lit a clove and inhaled the sweet poison. Tonight she wore jeans with a lavender sleeveless shell and black motorcycle boots. He was having a hard time reconciling that she could so quickly become a monster. Kathryn was mesmerizing, a strong woman and mother.

"So your last name is Spencer?" He asked, trying to lighten the mood at least for a moment.

"It is now. It has been since we got here. I was going to name myself after Evelyn Prentice, a Myrna Loy picture Paul took me to see not long after we arrived in America. He liked Hepburn-Tracy films better. Paul usually gets what he wants."

"Why does Dev hate Nathan so much, Kathryn?"

"Devrim has an attitude problem." Kathryn replied. "He's been carrying it around since Constantinople."

"I recognized that immediately, but I've seen Nathan attack twice in 48 hours. One of those attacks was on me."

"Nathan has troubles, Rube. He is beautiful, sensitive, and my baby boy but I don't pretend his issues don't exist."

"What kind of troubles?" Rube asked.

Kathryn deeply inhaled her clove then slowly exhaled. She looked at Rube.

"Nathan has blood lust." She said.

"Help me out, I'm new here. What does that mean?"

"Sometimes he can't help himself…he has to feed. My son is not a murderer so get that out of your mind. He has a compulsion; Paul thinks it might stem from the fever he had when he came over. It's why Paul brought him over. Nathan was dying of influenza, or what we thought might be influenza. He was such a sweet boy and I didn't want to see him suffer. Now he has this compulsion but his father helps."

"Feed?" Rube asked.

"What you see in the vampire movies? That's feeding."

Rube closed his eyes; that's what he was afraid of. He'd seen Kathryn drink blood since they met and assumed that her family did the same. The idea of them biting someone's neck and draining them of life made him nauseous. It also made him rethink his Taser idea.

"He hasn't had an incident in over a year." She said. "He and his father work so hard on it. With Paul gone I don't know what it will do to Nathan's recovery. To be perfectly honest, I can't even think about it right now. I have to keep my mind clear and focused."

"Alright," He nodded.

Rube didn't want to drop it but he did. Kathryn was carrying the weight of the world on her shoulders right now. Paul was missing and presumably in danger. Now there were other dangers that threatened her children. There would be no way of getting involved in one aspect of the disappearance of Paul Kirsch without getting knee deep in all the others. This wouldn't be something that he'd just be able to Google. Would it?

"It's raining out here, Kathryn. C'mon, I'll take you home."

She nodded, plucking the clove into the street and walking with Rube to his SUV. She could tell he had more questions but Kathryn didn't have the strength to answer tonight. She was quiet in the car, listening to Stevie Wonder on the radio. When he pulled up to the house, Rube got out of the car and went around to open the door for her. They went into the house together.

Nathan was sitting in the living room. He looked absolutely miserable but the FBI agent wasn't in the mood to give him the benefit of the doubt. Though he'd probably been alive, or undead, for many years he didn't look much older than 17 or 18. His pale skin and slightly sunken eyes did show a bit of illness.

But that also could've been stress from the loss of his father. It wasn't as if Rube was some kind of expert on what vampires looked like. Goddamn vampires…he needed to pinch himself. Again.

"Nath?"

"Mother, I was waiting for you to come back." He rushed into her arms.

"What's the matter?" Kathryn asked, running her fingers through his curly brown hair.

"I'm sorry." He curled his body into hers and Kathryn held him tight. "I'm so, so sorry."

"Oh Nath, my precious love; I know. We're all under immense pressure. Soon this will be nothing but a bad dream." She kissed his temple. "I promise you that."

"I'm going to bed but I was waiting for you to come back. I'm so tired."

"Sleep long and well. Is Johanna asleep?"

"I doubt it. She was annoying Charlie into reading her more fairy tales."

Nathan kissed his mother's lips and then said goodnight. Kathryn turned to Rube.

"Do you want to talk in the library?" She asked.

"Actually, do you think I could meet Johanna? I don't know how you would introduce me but…"

"I'll just tell her you're a friend of mine and Daddy's that's going to be around until he returns. We'll go up and see if she's still awake. Then we'll talk?"

"Yes, then we'll talk." Rube replied.

***

"I got quite a strange phone call a few days ago." Rube said.

"How strange?"

Rube was running around the American University track with Stephen Connelly, the junior Senator from New York. When they first met over a decade ago, Stephen was a big star on the rise in the Bureau. He had his eye on the Director's office one day until the sudden death of a popular New York Senator put him on a different path. With the full support of the DNC, the DCCC, and others in high places, Connelly won the seat in a landslide.

He was a third of the way through his second term. At 54, he looked to be running things on Capitol Hill for some time to come. Rube was very proud of his friend and told him so as often as he could. A lot of people said Stephen Connelly was his own worst enemy.

He was proving all the doubters wrong. You could have ambitions and morals, Stephen was a testament to that. He was by no means perfect, but he wasn't corrupt either. That never stopped people from trying to dig up hurtful things about him. Rube abhorred politics.

"There was a woman raving on my phone about the existence of vampires and secret government experiments taking place in the desert."

"I'm sorry?" Stephen looked at him with a raised eyebrow and they both laughed.

"Yeah. She called it Operation…I can't remember what she called it but she said vampires walk amongst us, are sanctioned by the government, and they are being used as guinea pigs to cure everything from the common cold to AIDS."

"Did you get a name?" Stephen asked. He slowed down a bit to watch two shapely coeds running in the other direction. He winked at one and she smiled. He'd try to catch up with her before she left.

"Oh I got plenty of names." Rube replied. "She said everyone from Michael Jordan and Tina Fey to Britney Spears and Colin Powell are vampires."

"I meant the name of the caller, Alex."

"No. I told her, as nicely as I could, to stop watching the X-Files and have a nice day."

"She told you Colin Powell was a vampire and you just let her hang up?" Stephen's tone was incredulous but he laughed.

"What was I supposed to do, Stef, put her through to the Director's office?"

"If I was the Director, the answer to that would've been a resounding yes. The one we have now would've just made it one of the best practical jokes of all time."

They kept running around the track in companionable silence, taking in the scenery around them. It was a lovely summer Saturday and the track was crowded with people who were happy for a break from the rain. This morning DC was sunny and blue. Who knew how long it would stay that way…they were in a swamp after all.

"You know what they say though?" Stephen asked, breaking the silence.

"What's that?" Rube glanced at him.

"Sometimes the folks spouting the most insane mumbo jumbo usually end up knowing the truth."

"Is that a direct quote?" Rube grinned. "Was that Voltaire?"

"You know what I mean, Alex?"

"I don't." he shook his head. "Am I supposed to? Are you telling me that Colin Powell is a vampire? Oh shit, is he? What kind of secrets do you learn when you join the U.S. Senate?"

"No. I'm just saying—last lap—lots of things exist in this world that we know nothing about. Sometimes they exist right under our noses."

"I'm willing to concede that point. I've seen my fair share of strangeness on this job. I have to draw the line at vampires. Do you believe…?"

"I just believe that I don't know everything." Stephen replied.

"I'm quoting you on that, Stef."

"You better not."

They ran the last lap, which made two miles, and then moved over to the bleachers to stretch their limbs.

"Nice necklace." Stephen's fingers toyed with the amulet. "Where did you get it?"

"A friend." Rube said.

"You have a friend, who buys you jewelry, and I'm just hearing about this? You haven't held out on me since the first Bush was in office."

"She's not that kind of friend, Stef. We um…she told me it was a good omen. She's Wiccan." Rube would've come up with a better lie in the interrogation room. He was a horrible liar with friends.

"If she's got you wearing a necklace," Stephen said. "She is that kind of friend. What's her name?"

"Kat. It's nothing special, really."

"Well I hope it is a good omen for you, kid. What are your plans for the rest of the afternoon?"

"I gotta drive out to Quantico. There's no rest for the wicked."

"I know what you mean. We need to have dinner sometime soon before I head back to Manhattan for a while." Stephen said. "You need to catch me up on what's happening in your life."

"It'll have to be fast food. I'm just a boring workaholic who occasionally gets intriguing phone calls." Rube replied.

"Tell me about it."

***

Dev walked down the badly lit alley, Morian at his side. He saw Rube before Rube saw him. He watched the FBI Agent light a cigarette and breathe a heavy sigh. His appearance oozed confidence but Dev saw rage, resignation, and sadness just below the surface of his heavy armor. He couldn't feel Rube's essence, he was human, but Dev had been around long enough to read most people at 50 paces. Alexander Rubidoux was a badass, in his lane. Here he was definitely feeling the strain.

"I'm glad I didn't go in." Rube said when Dev was in earshot. "I was looking for you."

"I don't usually come here, especially on a Saturday night. Too many goddamn vamps for my taste. But Max has some good cooks in the back and the female staff is easy on the eyes."

"You really hate vampires, don't you?"

"What's to like?" Dev replied.

"I don't know, Devrim, I'm a little over my head here."

"This ain't nothing like getting a coed back from a killer or some interstate custodial chase, is it?"

"Not really." Rube shook his head. "What if the government angle is the wrong angle? I'm not saying Operation: Eternity isn't real but what if we're chasing the wrong lead? I've wasted three days."

"I'll tell you this, Paul Kirsch has shady ass friends in the government. I wouldn't put any of this past him. They could've just killed him out right but that's not as easy as most would think."

"Well, I can't even question or corner people who know him because Kathryn is desperate to keep this quiet."

"No one really knows him. But you can question me if you'd liked." Dev said. "I'm far from Paul's inner circle but I've crossed paths with him and his family more times than I would like over the centuries."

"You don't seem to like him." Rube took a deep inhale of his cigarette. He hadn't had one in over five years. Tonight he stopped at the Circle K and bought a pack. If Kathryn found out, Rube would never live it down.

"I don't like a lot of people but I have a special disdain for vampires. Listen Rubidoux, they're soulless. If religion, philosophy, and mythology are to be believed souls house compassion, empathy, sympathy, faith; so many of the things that make us human. They're walking, talking sociopaths and Paul Kirsch is the oldest among them. He thinks and lives like a king."

"He seems like a dedicated family man." Rube said.

"I know Kathryn didn't tell you that." Dev made a face. "Did Kathryn tell you that?"

"Not exactly. But she wants him back for her and her children."

"She doesn't want to be slaughtered by Reapers for some stupid killing from 1917 that no one really gives a shit about. With dark hearts those bastards need little excuse to wreak havoc but having one is extra icing on the cake."

"I don't understand." Rube shook his head. He stubbed out the cigarette under his shoe and lit another. It was starting to drizzle again. "I need a little help here, Dev, with this supernatural shit. We don't have to be friends, but I need someone who isn't smack in the middle of this."

"Paul Kirsch is a powerful white man with near everlasting life in a powerful white man's world." Dev said. "There ain't nothing supernatural about that. He takes and devours all he wants, and that includes Kathryn. She's always been a woman, leaving her with little say and she was a bastard in aristocratic circles, which left her vulnerable. One bite and he owns her.

"I'm sure he wanted Halle for more than a daughter but his plan was somehow thwarted. Nathan was to be the boy king, there's one in every vamp family. Wars are usually started if there is two. I've seen that and it's not pretty. Paul thought that bite would cure whatever the kid had but it didn't. It probably just exacerbated the problem. Johanna was likely to pacify Kathryn in some way. Bloodsuckers rarely bite kids…they're baggage."

"Kathryn said that vampires are familial."

"How old are you?" Dev asked. "About 45, 50?"

"Give or take." Rube smirked.

"Your idea of familial and theirs is very different. Males bite females with the idea of taking them as sexual conquests and to draw in other members, like a cult almost. They bite no more than two, sometimes three, viral young men to continue their bloodlines. 3, 4, 500 years ago, vamps were a dime a dozen in Europe and Eurasia. But there are some dynastic families that go back to the time of Caesar. The world changed and they had to change with it or die out. Paul

Kirsch is a king without a throne, a court, and a royal family of loyal, obeying bloodsuckers.

"Rubidoux, this nuclear family bullshit that Kathryn tries to pull off while virtually being Paul's prisoner is bullshit. She should've left his ass when they finally escaped from Europe at the end of World War Two. He brought a black woman and three biracial vamplings who can't walk in the daylight to America in the goddamn 1940s and eventually settled in DC, which may as well be the South even though the North wasn't and isn't much better. That bastard knew what he was doing. Other than the shitty Reaper vendetta, his being gone is the best thing that could happen to her and those kids."

"Shit." Rube mumbled. That wasn't what he wanted to hear. No one was an angel but life with Paul Kirsch didn't sound like a picnic. He knew that Kathryn and her children were afraid of life without him but Rube wondered what life with him was like.

He probably did enough to get by as a father, though two of his children clearly had rage issues to spare. Kathryn showed signs of mistreatment but Rube couldn't imagine that she wouldn't after walking the earth for over 500 years as a black woman. He knew he would never be able to fathom her strength or her trauma. "Why are you helping them if he's such a bastard?"

"Three reasons. One, as much as I hate vamps, I know Ekaterina Petrova is a bad bitch and she just needs a swift kick of a reminder. Two, anyone who comes after kids, even bloodsucker kids, is on my list of things to annihilate. Three, Petrograd will be off the table forever and I'll be free of any perceived markers to the likes of Paul Kirsch."

"Who's Natalya, Devrim?"

"Paul's sister. They were bitten by the same vamp…blood of my blood and all. You think Halle is a hellion; Natalya would've eaten her for breakfast. She was slaughtering families, Rubidoux. She wasn't bringing people over or whatever, she was just draining them for the shits and giggles. There was a bounty on her head but Paul had pull and he was protecting her.

"He'll swear he wasn't, but he was. The bounty was nice but I would've killed the bitch for free. After the Great War, when the Council was finally established, they tried to make drinking only the law for vampires. As I said, the world was changing. You can't just go around slaughtering and biting people and think it wouldn't be noticed. Vamps are still fighting that law. In 2010 they're still fighting that law. Paul Kirsch is letting them."

"Who am I trying to bring back into the world?" Rube asked. He wanted to light a third cigarette but what he really needed was a stiff drink. Jesus. He didn't plan on going into Absinthe to get one.

"Look, man, pretty women in distress get us all the time. And I've heard she's an acrobat in bed, so, congrats, but..."

"I haven't slept with Kathryn Spencer."

"You haven't?" Dev raised an eyebrow.

"I'm an FBI agent doing my job and nothing more. I'm a kidnapping specialist and have been for over a decade. In your world that assumption doesn't seem to be offensive so I'm going to chalk it up to cultural differences and keep moving."

"It's probably for the best. You're a human so a female vamp in heat would probably rip your ass to shreds. Anyway, I got shit to do...don't have all night to chat it up with the likes of you. But I owe Kathryn so I'm going to keep my ear to the ground and help if I can. Be careful with that amulet, Jack Ryan, its worth more than you."

"So I've been told. Thanks for it, for what it's worth."

Dev nodded. He walked over to Absinthe's door, opened it, and he and his Rottweiler walked in. Even though his throat and chest ached, Rube lit a third cigarette as he walked back down the alleyway. It was quiet now but as the hour turned later more supernatural folks would be coming out to play. It was Saturday night in the nation's capital...there was a lot of sin to commit.

He wasn't in the mood to run into any of them. Rube would sit outside of Kathryn's house for an hour, make sure she and the children were safe before calling it a night. There was nothing else to do. He'd heard enough information tonight to make him want to say fuck Paul Kirsch.

Dev Hisham had a chip on his shoulder but Rube didn't think the immortal lied to him. Why Kathryn would want a life of subjugation and sadness to return, he really didn't know. What he did know was that she was a devoted mother to her children. And if survival of those children meant finding common ground with Paul then she would likely do it. She'd been doing it for half a millennia. He wasn't sure yet but maybe Rube could find her another option.

CHAPTER 3

Rube sipped the lukewarm coffee. It wasn't good but he'd surely had worse. The rain had finally slowed down; it had been pouring all day. He looked out the window. The waitress had been lingering for a bit but she finally gave up when her station filled with customers who actually wanted to eat. While Rube had perused the menu it was mostly for show…it was difficult to keep food down at the moment. A man slipped into the booth across from him; for a while they just stared at each other.

"Nice mustache." Rube said. "I didn't know Foghat was holding auditions for a new touring band."

"I'm trying out new looks." The guy said. "Life-like, isn't it?"

"Something like that."

They fell silence as the waitress approached. She poured coffee and was thrilled when he ordered a plate of hash browns and bacon. He wanted a lot of bacon. Rube just shook his head when she looked at him.

"Your guy has a lot of friends in high places, Rube."

"So I've heard. Any of these friends at Langley?"

"One or two, maybe. Most of the time we don't even know who's at Langley. But your guy knows people."

"Is he up to his eyeballs in something?"

"He's at least up to his pocketbook." He slid a napkin across the table.

Rube opened it and read it. He read it twice more, committing it to memory. Then he balled it up and dropped it in the water glass. That was a move straight out of the movies.

"You didn't hear a damn thing from me."

"I don't even know who you are." Rube shook his head. "It's real, isn't it?"

"I usually work on the assumption that every fuckin thing is real. Kirsch is involved in many things on his end and ours...he's important."

"I've seen him on C-Span; I figured that out. Wasn't it dangerous to make him disappear?"

"Sometimes one does what one has to, consequences be damned. Maybe they didn't count on his wife being so smart. It's not like he shows her off or anything. There are those who may be aware of her existence but not realize she is who she is. Hell, I know a lot and I can't pick Kathryn Spencer out in a lineup."

"That's a shame." Rube pushed the coffee cup aside. "I already like her better than him."

"Me too, and I don't even know her."

"How much do you know about him?"

"Not much I'm going to tell you." the guy replied, adding more sugar to his black coffee. "He's rich, powerful, and enigmatic. He's also a goddamn Quisling; sell his own folks up the river for money and God knows what else. He aint the first though."

"I don't want to know anymore." Rube sighed.

"Good, because I wasn't going to say anything. You sure you want him back?"

"His family does, and I have a job to do. Tell me if I'm looking for a man or a body."

"When he finally bites it, Rube, there likely won't be a body."

Nodding, the FBI Agent stood and walked away from the booth. He'd called in a huge marker for the little information that he received. It was going to have to do. The working theory by all was that Paul Kirsch was burned by those he was working with on covert government secrets. It was a wild theory and not easy to investigate. The information on that napkin made it just a little easier. He had to let Kathryn know.

***

Charlie let Rube in when he showed up at the house later that evening. He was holding a book of Dylan Thomas poems that looked to be a first edition.

"Good evening, Agent Rubidoux."

"Hello Charlie. How are you holding up?"

"I haven't gotten much sleep the past few days. I don't think any of us have except for Johanna. I've been doing everything I can to help Kathryn out right now with the children."

"I know you have. Is she here?"

"She's in the library."

"Thank you."

"Sure."

Charlie walked up the stairs with his book while Rube headed for the library. The doors were closed so he knocked and waited to hear Kathryn invite him in. He was surprised to see her looking so different from their past encounters. She was dressed in overalls, covered in dried pink paint. Her hair was in pigtails and she wore a camouflage scarf on her head. Paint splattered sneakers were on her feet. While Rube had taken Dev's advice and gone for a more casual look, black slacks and a lightweight blue sweater, this was something else entirely.

"Um…hi there."

"Hello, Alexander." She lit a clove and sipped something from a goblet. Rube assumed it was blood as he could see it on her lips. "Excuse my appearance, but Johanna and I were painting her playroom. I promised that we would today. Even in the midst of chaos, I don't like breaking promises to my little one. The break for levity was good for me as well. Can I offer you a drink?"

"As long as it's not what you're having." he managed a smile. This entire situation still boggled his mind but Rube was doing his best. That was pretty damn good considering.

"Do you prefer bourbon or scotch?" Kathryn asked.

"Bourbon. Do you keep liquor for visitors?"

"Paul is nearly 1200; he can eat and drink whatever he likes. His human business associates also prefer it. None of the rules really apply to him anymore. Even when they should have, I don't think they did."

Rube learned some of the rules the second night he and Kathryn talked. She told him that she was 576 years old, had passed most of the milestones already. At 200, reflections in mirror returned. She said that many vampires didn't make it to that age in her time. At 250, small portions of food could be consumed; most vampires preferred raw or nearly so. You could also be photographed once you reached that age; Kathryn found that out by accident. At 350, limited day walking was possible again; at 450 unlimited day walking.

At 500, vampires could eat larger portions of food. Being 1200, Rube could only assume that Paul Kirsch was practically human. Of course there was the issue of having no soul and craving blood. But at Paul's age, and even Kathryn's, Rube wasn't sure if it was a craving or just a means of survival.

"Sit down," Kathryn said going over to the mini-bar. "Please tell me your sources were able to give you something."

"Yes and no." Rube replied.

"I don't know what that means." She handed him the drink but didn't sit on the furniture.

"No one is going to tell me of the existence of vampires and covert government experiments, no matter how much they trust me, Kathryn. If they spilt the beans that easily they wouldn't have made it to top level security clearance. Still, I put out feelers and there is definitely something going on. I'm unable to get information on it but my experience in my job tells me it exists. I'm sorry I couldn't do more."

"Have you ever heard of Karen Pierson?" Kathryn asked.

Rube's whole demeanor changed. Pierson was career CIA…made people, places, and things disappear for a living. Some even doubted the existence of a woman by that name. If Paul Kirsch was in her clutches then he could be gone forever. Rube gave a solemn nod.

"It's strange that you've heard her name." He said.

"I told you that while I wasn't privy to all the details that Paul had some shady government associates. I think she was one of them."

"Pierson is rumored to be a cleaner…if such a person as Karen Pierson even exists. You know what I mean."

"I don't want to hear that, Alexander. I can't hear that right now. We are getting nowhere. Why aren't we getting anywhere? You're supposed to be the best. You brought that bank executive's children home when no one else could."

"I said I'd be upfront with you, I meant that. We're nowhere and I'm sorry but what am I supposed to do when we're talking about disappearing vampires and covert government conspiracies?"

"We don't have much time left." She replied. "Paul disappeared four days ago and we've managed to keep it under wraps but it won't be possible for much longer. There are whispers about someone powerful being taken. It's only a matter of time before a name is attached to the rumor."

"Who are you so afraid of, Kathryn?" Rube asked.

"I'm afraid of no one. Do you think I would still be walking this godforsaken earth if I scared so easily? I just don't want my children to be murdered for something that has nothing to do with them."

"Who would kill innocent children? Perhaps the Reapers you and Dev were whispering about?"

"Alex, you don't want to get involved in that. Just stay outside and work the kidnapping." Kathryn said.

"It only took me a couple of days to figure out that there is no outside in this case. Talk to me, Kathryn. Please. I'm in this; I'm in it and I plan to see it through to the end. You can trust me. I know from experience that that's asking a lot but please. Trust me."

She looked at him as she sighed and finally sat down on the couch. This was exhausting…the whole thing was too much to carry. Maybe it was time to share the load. She couldn't explain why but she did trust him. Her gut never steered her wrong, though there had been times she refused to listen.

Alexander Rubidoux was, thus far, a man of his word. If he said he would help then he would help. That didn't mean they would succeed in this clusterfuck of a case, but he had her back. Kathryn wished she could tell him how much that meant to her. It had been so long, she almost forgot what being able to fall back felt like.

"We lived in Petrograd at the time of the Bolshevik Revolution." She lit a clove with the remnants of another. "Both Paul and I are from Russia originally and though we traveled for centuries, all over Europe, Asia, and North Africa, at the time Petrograd was our home together. You can imagine the insanity there if you've read about it in a history book but it was doubly so because there was also a war going on in our world. It was easy to hide amongst all the Bolshevik slaughter.

"Lots of things happened, things I don't need to get into, but Charlie was attacked in an alley one night by a Reaper named Julian Black. He was nearly killed and Paul killed Julian in defense. It was a terrible time; lots of innocent people died in The Darkness' reign for supremacy over the light. After Julian was killed, his family vowed revenge. That's how it's done in our world, Alexander; an eye for an eye. Except there are those for whom one bloodletting will never be enough."

"So you think that the Reapers will come and try to kill you?" Rube asked.

"I don't think, I know. Once they catch an inkling of Paul being gone and our perceived vulnerability, they will come for us. Marin won't stop until he kills my children and Charlie as well. In a just world, which has never existed, Paul would be his only target. Instead he and his clan intend to get him where it will hurt the most."

"I won't let him." He shook his head. "We'll get him first."

"I appreciate your tenacity, Alexander, but you have no idea what you're up against. We've been hiding in this house for so long I had almost forgotten how brutal it is out there. This is a position that

I've never been in and I hardly know how to function from day to day. I feel I only have myself to blame for becoming so complacent."

Rube didn't know how to comfort her. He didn't like the idea of a hopeless situation; something could always be done. He may not know a damn thing about Reapers or some of the other creatures that inhabited her world but he knew he wouldn't back down. Children weren't going to die on his watch and neither would Kathryn Spencer.

He'd had hard cases before; had seen all of them through. This one would be no different. While there weren't always happy endings, it wasn't because Rube didn't give 150%. Taking a deep breath, he reached for her. His hand landed on her upper arm so he just rubbed. Kathryn gave him a soft smile, putting her hand over his.

"I have a possible lead."

"What the hell, Rube? You could've started with that instead of making it seem so hopeless. Why are you holding out on me?"

"Well, I…" Rube didn't know what to say. Firstly, she called him Rube, which she never had before. Secondly, she was right but he was trying to get information. You don't get information by handing over the best card in your deck as soon as you sit at the table. "I have a friend, a friend at Langley who owes me a big favor. Even with that, doing what he did could get us all in a lot of trouble.

"He did it anyway. There are five possible facilities in the United States where the government could be conducting secret experiments and a plethora of other things none of us really want to know about. There is one on the border of Maine and Canada, one in the Florida Everglades, and a facility in Palmerton, Pennsylvania. Another facility is in Fulton, Kentucky and the fifth is somewhere around the DC corridor. He refused to give me the exact location. Paul has to be in one of them."

"How do you know this?" Kathryn asked. "They could've carried him off to Bucharest by now."

"It's probable but not likely. If they're working on the key to eternal life, which is ridiculous enough, surely they want dibs. If they travel with him to another country, they would be forced to share some kind of information with others. They don't want to do that. Moving him too far wouldn't be a smart move. It would involve too many people and too many secrets. I'm going to take this information, share it with someone I trust, and we might be able to find out where Paul is."

"Wait, Alexander, don't give away too much. If someone feels the heat is on they might move him; or worse."

"I don't trust many people. If I'm going to help you, you have to trust me a little. If you can't then there's no reason for me to be here. You have to let me work it in the ways that I know how."

Kathryn nodded, walking over to the table and lighting another clove. After this was all over she would send the children away so she could cleanse and air out the house. Smoke lingered in the air like something in a Vincent Price film.

"You know that's an awful habit...you should probably quit."

"Because it could kill me, right." She replied rolling her eyes. "You don't have to hide it from me, Alexander; I smelled the tobacco on your collar last night. So unless you like to solicit smoking hookers you've been sneaking a few as well."

"No comment." Rube mumbled. "Especially on the smoking hookers thing."

"I'm going to change into something more presentable."

"Sure. I'm going to make a phone call."

"I'll leave you to it."

He watched her walk out of the room. Rube took his phone from his pocket. He pressed four and listened to it ring. A bubbly voice answered.

"Hey, hey, hey."

"Hello, Jules."

"Well I feel pretty special cuz it's Sunday. What can I do for you on the day of rest in which you're clearly not resting and neither am I?"

Rube gave Jules most of the information he'd just given Kathryn.

"I'm going to need you to dig up anything you can on these places. Legal and…otherwise."

"But you told me that you didn't like otherwise." She replied. "You told me like just last week."

"Right now I don't have the time to be so picky. All of your considerable expertise is needed." Rube said.

"Can you tell me what this is for, Sir?" Jules asked. She knew vague things about secret government facilities so she thought it strange that a by the book FBI agent like Alexander Rubidoux was asking her to dig into them. He seemed out of his element. She wondered whose element he was in.

"I can't Jules, but I need you to be very careful. Every back door you go through needs to be left just as you found it. I need you to be a ghost; this request is off the grid."

"You've never been an off the grid kinda guy, Boss."

"Tell me about it." Rube mumbled.

"Are you alright? I can help with any kind of computer work you need but do you need services that perhaps I can't provide?"

Rube raised an eyebrow though his favorite government employed hacker couldn't see that over the phone. He wanted to know what she meant by that.

"You know me; I know lots of people in lots of places. I've lived in this city a long time. A long, long time." Jules said. "If you're off the grid then I know people who can help. I'm telling you that you can't do off the grid on your own. For example, you're not even calling me from a secure line or burner cell. You've broken like 395 rules already."

"Jules, what I am about to say may be the craziest thing that even you've ever heard." Rube trusted her, period. He needed to be able to say it aloud to someone, even if it was just so he could finally say it aloud to himself. "How would you feel if I told you that vampires exist and live amongst us? Not just vampires though, but probably damn near everything we thought were myths or figments of our imaginations?"

"I'd feel pretty secure since I already knew that. What are you into, Sir? I have a friend and he handles things like this. I don't want you getting hurt; he can handle it without asking too many questions. His fees are exorbitant but he owes me so I'm sure I can get him to take on a little pro bono work."

"What's his name?" Rube asked.

"Dev." She said.

"Devrim Hisham?"

"You know Dev?" It was impossible for Jules to hide the shock in her tone. If Rube was involved with Dev then off the grid was an understatement.

"I need you to hang up the phone. Hang up the phone Jules, grab two laptops, and come to the address I'm going to give you."

After ending the phone call, Rube walked out of the library and ran into Halle. Something about the way the young woman looked at him made him so uncomfortable. He wasn't sure if she wanted to fuck him, eat him, or kill him for the hell of it. She had a warrior's eyes. He had no idea how old she was but he could imagine her riding on a horse through some desolate field of bodies in some ancient European city after taking heads.

Like she fought at the side of Hannibal or Germanicus or any of those other warriors Rube didn't always pay attention to lessons about in history class. She was also stunningly beautiful. The polar opposite of her mother in looks, he could only imagine the damage those two could do in a room full of men. And it had nothing to do with fangs and claws.

"Is there any news on my father, Agent Rubidoux?" She asked.

"Nothing concrete but we're getting closer by the minute."

"If I didn't know any better I would think you were just here to be closer to my mother. You don't seem to be doing anything else."

"You couldn't be more wrong." Rube shook his head. "I'm doing my job, Halle."

"I read up on you; you're supposedly the best in the Bureau." She looked him up and down, crossing her arms over her chest. "They say you're some kind of specialist. The best can't find one missing person in four days. Perhaps you've been oversold."

"Your father was likely kidnapped by people he was in cahoots with in the first place. Do you think they would make it easy to find him?"

"How do I know you weren't involved in his kidnapping? Why would some government suit want to help us anyway?" Brimstone flashed in Halle's green eyes. "I want you to know that I'm watching you. My mother may think you're worth your salt but I don't trust you. And when my father returns I'm going to tell him about all of this. I won't allow you to take my mother into your bed during her time of emotional duress."

"I promise you that I'm doing everything in my power to bring him home. That's the only agenda I have. And I'm not sleeping with your mother." Rube said wondering why sex seemed to be a given amongst this crowd. "I don't even know where she is at the moment."

"Don't pretend you've never been in her bedroom, Agent Rubidoux. I'm not Johanna; I know men have wants. I'm not a baby."

"Then stop acting like one."

"Don't talk to me like that!" she moved closer to him, fangs and nails out. "I could tear you limb from limb without breaking a sweat."

Rube backed up, pulled out his Glock, and took off the safety. He knew the rules; never pull your weapon unless you intended to use it. He hadn't in some time, just being a badass had been enough to get by. He wasn't a badass here…they were all monsters. Rube didn't like thinking about it in that way but truthfully, how was he supposed to survive being on the bad side of something like that without serious firepower backup.

"I will fuckin shoot you." he said, sounder calmer than he felt. "I may not kill you but it's going to hurt like hell. I will shoot you, Halle. Back off!"

"Just try it." She growled, taking another step forward. "Fuckin shoot me. Try it and see!"

Rube steadied his stance. He kept telling himself that it wouldn't kill her, it might actually piss her off more. But she wouldn't die. His finger was on the trigger and ready to go.

"Back off, Halle. What's the matter with you?"

She looked up at Nathan standing on the stairs. Hissing at him, she turned and stormed into the library. Rube breathed a sigh. He still held his stance for a few more moments, unsure what to expect.

"Nathan, where is your mother?" Rube slowly lowered his Glock, his eyes still trained on the library door.

"In her bedroom. If you go to the top of the stairs and turn left, it's at the top of the hall. She has the master suite."

"Can you please come down so I can go up?"

"Are you going to shoot me, Agent Rubidoux?"

The fear in his voice made Rube look at him. Damn, he looked like a scared kid. He was a scared kid, a kid who had blood lust and sometimes drained the life from people. Christ, Rube was in over his head.

"Of course not." He holstered his weapon. "I would just feel better, alright. I'm not going to hurt you; I promise. Come on down."

Nodding, Nathan came down the stairs. He moved off to the side and let Rube go past. The FBI agent took the stairs two at a time. For the first time in almost 96 hours, Rube felt as if they were getting somewhere and he didn't need anything pulling the rug from under his already unsteady feet. Knocking on the door and then walking in, he found Kathryn topless. Water glistened off her skin; she wiped some away with a hand towel. Kathryn didn't bother to hide her nudity and light caught the surgical steel horseshoe piercings in both of her nipples.

Rube also saw the circular silver metal mesh that covered her heart. She told him that her whole family wore them to protect them from staking. It was nearly impossible for wood to penetrate it. As he stared at her, and Rube found it quite difficult not to, he couldn't help but wonder how it stayed on her skin.

"I'm so…" He finally got his wits, mostly, and tried to back out of the room. His shoulder blade hit the doorframe pretty hard instead. He let out a groan of frustration and pain. "I didn't mean to…uh…Kathryn…you're…"

He didn't know why he couldn't just turn his eyes away from her. Was that the lure they used to trap humans or was she truly the beauty his eyes beheld? The dark skin of her body was just as flawless as her face. Her breasts were full, perfect, and her nipples erect. His body reacted to her body; there was nothing Rube could do about it.

Is this what Halle assumed was going on as her father possibly languished somewhere in a sterile government facility? Kathryn threw the towel on the bed. She reached for the black tee shirt on her bed, pulling it over her head. She didn't seem to be paying his stammering and nervousness much mind. Her hair was still in pigtails.

"Are you hungry, Alexander?" She asked as if she wasn't topless mere seconds before. "Nathan is making me filet mignon and I would be happy to share. It's been months since I've eaten so forgive my excitement. I can have him cook yours to your liking."

"No," Rube shook his head. "Um, no thank you. I'm not that hungry and Nathan's cooking so…"

"He's actually quite good at it."

"A vampire chef?" he smirked. "I've already taken in enough new information. I don't know if I can handle much more tonight. We'll give it a go tomorrow."

"Nathan enjoys cooking; enjoys the sounds and smells of food. It's important to his father and me that we put his boundless mental energy into something constructive. We both feel…"

"Halle attacked me." Rube cut her off. He didn't even get a chance to apologize before Kathryn was rushing to his side.

"Alexander, are you alright? Did she hurt you?" like a mom, she began to inspect him for bites and scratches. Halle could be vicious when she was mad. Rube wasn't of their world; she could really hurt him. Just because he couldn't die while wearing the amulet didn't mean she couldn't mangle him for life. "Dammit, I am so, so sorry."

"I don't mean to sound judgmental, but your children have some rage issues. More than once since I started working this case it's been directed at both me and you. I don't have the means to fight them, Kathryn. I would have to shoot my way out of the situation and that's only a short term escape. For all I know it could just piss them off more."

"Did she hurt you?" Kathryn asked again. She was trying to settle her own rage. For so long they'd been cooped up in this house, forced to make nice with each other for survival. The prison gates had been left unlocked and now the monsters inside had taken over. She worried that it would be hard to quiet them if and when things ever returned to normal.

"She's very angry that we haven't found Paul yet." Rube replied. He stepped to the side some, away from her hands. It felt wonderful and uncomfortable at the same time to be pawed by her. Surely it was better than being pawed by her daughter. "Halle can't decide if that's because I'm one of the people who kidnapped him or if you and I are having an illicit affair and don't want him back."

"Did she say that to you?" Kathryn's eyes turned black.

"Please don't vamp out on me." He held up his hands in defense. "I've had enough of that this evening."

"I'm sorry. My daughter is extremely temperamental. She is fiercely devoted to her father…any and everyone is competition. She probably wouldn't care if we were fucking so long as you didn't think you were going to replace Paul. It's so goddamn tiring."

"Don't apologize for her behavior. Its noble but she's damn sure old enough to know better. I don't care if she's mad, I just don't want to be attacked. I don't want you to be attacked."

"Halle would never."

"Are you sure about that?" Rube asked. "Nathan did; under duress or not."

"Don't make me doubt one of the few things I think I have to hold onto." Kathryn closed her eyes. "My children are blood of my blood…but I did not sire them. We share familial blood but mine doesn't course through their veins. They came over with their own thoughts, personalities, struggles, and yes Alexander, even their rage.

"Nothing is perfect in this family. I try to protect them and may even coddle them a bit too much. I've been a mother for a long time but that doesn't mean I can't stand to learn some lessons. I will talk with Halle. I'm not saying it will help, but I will speak with her."

"Can I ask you something?"

"Yes." Kathryn nodded. She was actually tired of answering questions but it hardly mattered anymore.

"How old were you when…what do you call it?" Rube leaned against the wall, was finally starting to get his bearings.

"You want to know how old I was when Paul brought me over."

"Yes." Rube said.

"I was in my mid-30s, which is 60 by today's standards. I had a better chance than most being born into aristocracy though most looked at me as little more than a bastard after my parents died. Something as simple as a cut or a sniffle could mean a long, painful death where I'm from. Maybe I'm just deluding myself when I think I didn't know exactly what Paul, who was Pavel then, meant offering me forever in his embrace. I would've sold my soul to get out of there. That's exactly what I did.

"I'm sure there are worst places than Tsarist Russia, I've been to some of them, but times were hard. I was forced into marriage by my aunt at 17, a mother at 18, a mother again at 19, and a pregnant widow at 22. My Aunt wanted me to remarry quickly but I refused. I was of dark skin and to most of those men I was nothing more than a fetish despite my aristocratic bloodline. I did not want to be another rich man's sex slave. I'd grown fond of my husband Sasha, who respected me as much as any man would in that time...I wanted time to mourn the loss. Uncle conceded because my dowry and family name made me a worthwhile catch at almost any time."

"What happened to your children?" Rube asked.

"Baby Grigori died a few hours after his birth; I named him after my father. Little Sasha was four when a fever and fits took him. My Lilia lived past her tenth birthday but then plague came...she was my oldest. She had become the center of my world and losing her was difficult. By the time Pavel came into my life I was just waiting to die too.

"He offered me an alternative. Oh God," Laughing nervously, Kathryn ran her hands over her face. "I'm sorry; you probably didn't want to hear my whole sad story. Honestly, it's likely been a century since anyone asked me where I came from. I don't often get to speak of home. The memories are incredibly fuzzy and for that I am most grateful. Where are you from, Agent Rubidoux?"

"I was born in Lynchburg, Virginia but moved to Richmond with my family when I was four years old. I lived in Richmond until I left for college outside of Philadelphia. I guess by most standards I'm a typical Southern boy."

"You don't have one of those Southern accents, like the good old boys in the movies." Or the ones who burned crosses on her lawn less than four decades ago.

"With hard work, one can lose it over time. It manifests in the strangest ways every once in a while. You don't sound very Russian to me."

"You've never heard me speak my native tongue." Kathryn replied, managing a small smile. "Did you need anything else? Is something happening?"

"My friend is on her way here." Rube replied. "I trust her wholly and she's going to help us."

"Who is this person, Alexander? How will she help?"

It was hard for Kathryn to hide her discomfort. Now someone had her address and was on their way to her home, where her children were. Rube asked her to trust him and Kathryn was doing the best that she could. Despite a bumpy start, they worked well together. She had less fear and more drive since she convinced him to help her. Whether they succeeded or failed was anyone's guess but they wouldn't give up. It had been a long time since Kathryn felt like part of a real, mutually beneficial partnership.

"Her name is Jules Sohn." He said. "She knows more about everything than anyone I've ever met."

"You and I have very different definitions of everything you know." Kathryn said.

"Well, when it comes to Jules, I'm starting to think she might cover the whole spectrum."

000

"OK, little kiddos, how about some formal introductions. My name's Jules, what's yours?"

They all watched Jules move around the library like a whirling dervish. She was turning on, plugging in, tweaking, and building. For what she needed to do everything had to be set up just right.

"I'm Charlie." he waved from the corner. He'd let her into the house and had been staring at her ever since. She was a fascinating creature in her yellow polka dot pants and spring green sweater, buttoned at the neck like a 50s housewife. Her hair was bright red and cut in a fashionable bob.

"How are you, Charlie? Cool sweater...argyle cardigans are making a comeback."

"Thanks," He smiled. "I like yours too."

"My name's Halle. I'm the eldest and most interesting of them all."

"Nice to meet you, Halle. One day I'll let you regale me with stories of your awesomeness, I promise."

"I'm Johanna...you wanna see my fangs?"

"Aww, you are too cute for words." Jules said. She tugged on one of Johanna's thick brown curls. She had thousands of them.

"Johanna, you shouldn't show your fangs to strangers." Halle told her.

"Don't worry about it," Jules replied. "I've seen worse."

"That's Nathan," Johanna pointed behind Jules. "He's lurking."

Jules turned around and smiled at the boy. He was pacing, didn't looked quite agitated but something was off.

"Hello, Nathan."

"Your food smells really good." He said.

"Yeah, I stopped at Sonic on the way over here. Hackers cannot work on just their good looks alone. Know what I mean?"

"It smells delicious." His eyes flashed black.

"A vampire with a taste for burgers? Now I've seen it all." Jules sat down in the chair, turning on her laptops. "So, Johanna, let's see those pointers."

The eight year old roared like a lion, opening her mouth and exposing her sharp teeth. Jules clapped.

"That's awesome! You really are too cute for words."

"Thank you." Johanna curtsied.

Nathan walked around in front of Jules. His attention was still focused on her dinner bag. She wasn't paying him much mind.

"Do you think you could share?" He asked. "I don't eat very much…and it smells so good."

"Oh my God," Halle rolled her eyes. "You are such a little savage."

"Shut up, you hateful shrew." Nathan's voice went deep as he hissed and flashed his fangs at her.

"Hey guys," Charlie intervened. "Could we try to at least act civilized in front of guests?"

"Nathan?" Jules got his attention.

"Huh?"

"How old are you, kid?"

"285 in November." He replied.

Jules pulled the tater tots from her bag.

"Have a few but don't tell your mom."

He smiled, bringing his fangs into full view. Grabbing some from the paper box, Nathan devoured them. He sighed.

"Oh my God, they are so good." The words came slowly out of his full mouth.

"Only the best for my temple," Jules replied. "Know what I mean?"

"I totally do." he nodded.

Kathryn and Rube walked into the library while Nathan was still licking salt from his lips. Jules stood from the chair.

"Hey, Mommy!" Johanna ran to her mother's arms.

Kathryn smiled, picking her up and holding her close. Rube saw another side of her when she was with her children. He'd judged her in the beginning but had been wrong. He hadn't been there when decisions were made that impacted her and her family. This was her life now and Kathryn Spencer was a loving mother, no doubt about that.

Anyone could see that and Rube did too. It just made him more determined to find Paul Kirsch and keep his family safe. What happened after that he wasn't sure? Rube would cross that bridge when he got to it. It was better to work one obstacle at a time.

"Hi, I'm Jules Sohn." As usual, Jules wore an easygoing smile.

"Hello," Kathryn walked over, took Jules's hand, and bowed her head. "It's an honor to have you in my home, Jules. You will bring the light."

"I hope so." She replied.

"What light?" Rube asked. "Am I missing something?" He felt as if he was missing something. The whole aura of the room had just changed. *Oh God*, he thought, *now I'm thinking about auras. Holy hell.*

"Jules is an augur." Kathryn said, looking back at Rube.

"I don't know what that means, Kathryn."

"Well the dictionary definition of an augur," Charlie said from his spot by the bookshelves. "Is to divine or predict, as from omens; prognosticate. That means Jules knows all, sees all, and will tell all if asked properly."

Rube looked at Jules with his mouth slightly open. He'd known her for eight years, considered her a friend. They spent time together outside of work, not tons of time but time nonetheless. He bought her Christmas gifts, knew the strange music she liked, and loved to listen to stories of her grandmother acting up at the retirement community where she lived.

Jules Sohn was a breath of fresh air compared to those he spent all day with. Rube was surrounded by white guys in suits with guns. Jules was a woman, she was Korean-American, and she hated guns. Jules was his friend. Now he wasn't sure if he'd ever known her at all. Not Jules... not this.

"How long do augurs live?" He asked.

"We're immortal," she replied. "Though everyone dies eventually. You know?"

"No, Jules, I don't know. I went to your 30th birthday party last October." Rube reasoned.

"It was my third 30th birthday, Boss."

"Of course it was, but women are allowed to have more than one 30th birthday. I wasn't going to ask about it and get myself in trouble. What about Grandma Sohn, Jules? And Bashira, you said that you and Bash had been together forever. Did you really mean forever? Oh my god."

"One thing at a time." Jules sat back in the chair and worked on her computers. "You can't possibly think you're going to be able to soak this all in right at the moment."

"Johanna, love," Kathryn said. "It's time for bed."

"But I wanna stay with the augur, Mommy. I was showing her my fangs."

"You need some sleep; it's been a long day. No arguments."

The child pouted but was quickly pacified by her mother's kisses.

"And this kiss is from Daddy." Kathryn kissed her nose.

"When is Daddy coming home?" Johanna asked. "He hasn't even called me. He always calls when he's far away."

"He should be home to you very soon."

"I miss him a lot."

"You go with Charlie, and no more than one chapter of reading tonight." Kathryn kissed her once again, putting her down. "Sweet dreams."

"Goodnight, Mommy. Goodnight, Agent Rube; goodnight, Jules."

"Goodnight, sweetie pie." Jules waved.

"Guys, Alexander and I need to talk to Jules alone. Would you excuse us?"

Nathan nodded, following Charlie and Johanna out of the room. Halle just stood there giving Rube the dagger eyes.

"I'm really sick of being pushed out of rooms, Mother." She said. "I'm sure I can be more helpful than this so-called FBI agent. At least I give a damn about Daddy. I don't think he's on our side at all. Did he tell you that he pulled his gun on me earlier?"

"You threatened to tear me limb from limb, Halle." Rube countered. The little bitch. "Nathan witnessed the entire thing. Shall we bring him back in here?"

"Alexander is helping, but you're not by constantly pushing my buttons or his" Kathryn said. "We have this under control; we don't need you bringing in emotional upheaval. The state you're in right now, Halle, is of no use to anyone."

"But, why does he…?"

"In the time we're wasting your father could be killed! Leave this room, you petulant brat!" Kathryn exclaimed.

Halle jumped at the sound of her mother's anger. She bit her lip and tears filled her eyes as blood slid down her chin. She had bitten her lip with a fang

"I hate the way you're acting! Don't separate your essence from ours." Halle tried to hold back her tears. "Alexander Rubidoux isn't blood of our blood. Don't let him keep us from Daddy."

"Please stop this childish attempt to control everything. You have no idea what you're talking about and this behavior is hurting, not helping." Kathryn walked over to her daughter and gently wiped the blood from her chin. Then she pressed her forehead to Halle's. "Alexander brought this augur to us. He is on the trail of where your father is right now. He's here to help."

"I can hardly feel Daddy anymore." Halle whispered, clutching her stomach. "That frightens me."

Kathryn wouldn't admit it aloud, but she was starting to feel farther and farther away from Paul as well. For her it wasn't as desolate a feeling as it was for Halle. Still, Kathryn wouldn't wish the void on anyone. She took a deep breath.

"He will return to us."

"How can you be sure?"

"If his essence ceases to be, I would surely know it." Kathryn replied. "Have I ever lied to you, Halle Annah?"

Halle shook her head, allowing Kathryn to wipe errant tears from her cheek. She excused herself and walked out of the room. Kathryn sat down on the couch near Jules. She watched her fingers quickly moving over the keyboard. She looked into the augur's eyes.

"You know how this is going to end, don't you?" Kathryn asked. "You know if we'll succeed or fail…if Paul lives or dies."

"I know many things," Jules replied, looking at her. "None of which I can discuss with you at this time. Events change every second based on choices, decisions, and conversations; including this one. I'm here to use my other formidable skills to help this turn out as you want it to. There are many different ways to bring calm to the chaos within this family."

Kathryn nodded. She got up and walked over to the window, pulling back the heavy curtain to look out. Another night was falling in the nation's capital. It was another night with Paul out there somewhere and not home with his children. What would she tell them if the mission failed? They could survive without him, but Kathryn was concerned that Paul hadn't made provisions for them to do so. She had a lot of work to do when this was all said and done. Paul or no Paul, it was time for some major changes in the life she lived.

"I appreciate everything you're doing, Jules." Rube said.

"It's not a problem, Boss, believe me. I want to help in any way I can. Kids missing their daddy breaks my heart."

Rube walked over to where Kathryn stood but kept some distance between them. He crossed his arms.

"You know what never changes?" She asked. "People in positions of authority always think they have the right to control and toy with the lives of others. Of all the things that should be different after 500 years, it should've been that. I have no idea how I will look into the eyes of my children if I can't fix this."

To him that sounded like Paul Kirsch from what little he could glean about the man and the situation. Rube sighed, stepping forward and putting both hands on her shoulders. She was so warm; he didn't know how it was possible. He associated dead with cold. Undead was still dead, right? Shouldn't she be cold? Her heat made him squeeze just a little tighter.

"We're going to save Paul." He said.

Kathryn leaned back on him, felt his hard chest on her back. She wasn't sure it was the best idea but she had to lean on someone. She was strong, but it was ridiculous to think she could do this alone. Rube was risking so much and didn't even know her.

Four days ago he didn't think he wanted to. So much had changed in just four days. Kathryn needed to stop trying to make sense of it and just get through it. She had gotten through hell, more times than anyone should have to. She would get through this too.

"Don't make me promises that you can't keep, Agent Rubidoux. I'll never die and I have quite a long memory." Kathryn tried to smile but didn't quite make it.

"I mean it, Kath." Rube replied, the name slipping from his lips as if he'd called her that a million times before. He massaged her shoulders and thought he felt her relax under his touch.

"Guys," Jules called from across the room. "I think I just reeled in a shark."

CHAPTER 4

"Nathan?"

"Huh?" he turned, saw Rube, and stepped back against the bannister. His eyes immediately found his shoes. "Yes, Agent Rubidoux?"

Nathan was an enigma to Alex. He'd seen him vamp out, and that was scary as hell. He knew that he injured his mother out of anger and fear…Rube didn't witness the event, only the aftermath. But most of the time he was a shy, demure young man. Halle liked to push his buttons but she did that with everyone.

It didn't seem as if Nathan wanted to bring any unnecessary attention to himself. Stay quiet, keep your head down, and love your mother. Jesus, Rube was looking at himself. It was how some emotionally abused and neglected kids behaved. He didn't isolate himself like Nathan did, at least not externally, but Nathan had good reason.

If he stepped out in the sunlight, he would likely spontaneously combust…or something. He was trapped in this house; trapped in his life. Despite what he'd seen and heard, Rube felt sorry for the kid. Maybe he could use that empathy to get some answers.

"I want to apologize for what happened earlier." Rube said. "With your sister."

"Father calls her his little spitfire. I think of it more as hellfire but she doesn't treat him like she treats me."

"I wondered if I could talk to you about that."

"About Halle?" Nathan asked. He almost managed to look Rube in the eye.

"About your family; your father. Only if you want to."

"You're not going to interrogate me like the police on television, are you? Did you know they can actually lie to people to get information? Then lawyers say that lying is OK to get the criminals. How is that OK when you then take an oath in court to be honest? You have to touch the Bible, which implies that you are swearing to God. But I guess people lie then too. It's not as if the Bible means something to everyone. I've read some of it but I'm not a follower. Are they called followers?"

"Mostly they're called Christians." Rube replied.

"People use religion to harm more than to help." Nathan said. "Look at the Salem Witch Trials or the Holocaust. There was also a vampire purge in Eastern Europe and Eurasia during the Great War. Whole families were wiped out. They said it was done to eradicate the soulless."

"I can't argue about people using religion for all the wrong reasons. Do you mind if we talk a little bit? No interrogation, I promise."

"Alright." Nathan nodded. He sat down in one of the wrought iron chairs. "I want to help you find my father if I can. I don't know much but I want to try."

"How old are you, Nathan? If you're under a certain age then your mother should probably be here."

"I'm 284 years old, Agent Rubidoux…I think we're OK."

"But how old were you when…?" Rube didn't quite know how to say it. He didn't know how much Nathan might remember of his past life and he certainly didn't want to bring up anything that might upset him.

"I was a few months past my 18th birthday. I had gotten sick, they called it a respiratory illness. The doctors didn't hold out much hope. I was weak, was going to end it myself so not to put the burden on my caretakers or spread the illness. My father offered me another option, a life without sickness. It didn't quite turn out that way."

Nathan held back his sigh but his bluish-green eyes were downcast. He hadn't thought about his origins in a long time. This life was supposed to be better but the road to hell was paved with good intentions.

"Tell me a little about your father. Does he have a lot of friends?"

"I don't know. He has business partners and there would be meetings or dinner parties here sometimes. He's such a busy man. I guess he didn't have time for frivolous things. Work, and the benefits it reaps, are very important to him."

"How much time did he spend with you and your sisters?" Rube asked.

"We were closer when we traveled Europe as a family." Nathan replied. "We were around more people like us, more clans. Mother was happier and we didn't feel as isolated, even traveling mostly by darkness. I understand why we left but nothing was ever the same."

"What about enemies, Nathan? Does your father have enemies?"

"Of course he does. He doesn't talk about it with us but he's walked the earth for a very long time. The work he does with finance upsets some people. He is a leader in the Council and I know he's gotten death threats before. Mother tries to keep it quiet but I still overhear things. I don't eavesdrop, Agent Rubidoux."

"I believe you." Rube smiled some. "Can you tell me what your parents' relationship is like? Are they close? Are they not close?"

"I don't know what you mean." Again, Nathan was looking at his feet.

"Does your father love your mother?"

"Yes."

"Has he ever yelled at her or hit her in anger?" Rube asked.

"I don't think the police should know our personal family business." Nathan replied.

Well that was definitely not a no. If the answer was no than Nathan would've said no. Rube knew nothing about the dynamics of vampire families, except what Dev told him. It was clear that men ruled the roost. Perhaps abuse was seen as normal and not as abuse.

That was unacceptable to Rube. But he promised not to interrogate Nathan. The line he was walking right now was quite fine. There weren't many ways Nathan could help him with this case. He was mostly trying to figure out what was the deal with this family.

"I don't want to invade your personal family life."

"I watch crime shows on television and read books. They always blame it on the wife if the husband disappears. My mother would never hurt my father and she's not a part of his life outside of our home. She loves us very much and knows that we need him in our lives. She has sacrificed everything to be a good mother. None of this is easy for her, Agent Rubidoux."

"What's hard for your mother, Nathan?"

"Life with my father." He replied. "I don't know anything else."

Rube knew that wasn't the truth but it was time to end this. None of it would bring Paul Kirsch back to his family. He was just desperate to see the light in this case. Rube knew nothing and he wasn't fond of the feeling. If this big lead led him to Paul then he was still just as clueless about a case he was immersed in. And the idea of actually placing Kathryn Spencer and her children back in a clearly toxic, possibly abusive situation made Rube both angry and nauseous.

"Do you have any more questions for me, Agent Rubidoux?"

"Not right now, Nathan, though I appreciate you talking to me. I know how worried and upset you are. All of this has caused a lot of upheaval in your life."

"Are you going to find my father alive?" Nathan asked. "I'm not a little kid like Johanna, you can be honest with me."

"The honest truth is that I don't know. We have leads and I'm working very hard. Your mother is too. This is what I do for a living, Nathan, I find missing people. I'm very good at it but I don't solve every case."

"Whatever happens, my mother will take care of us."

"Damn straight." Rube said.

"What does that mean?"

"It means that's exactly what she's going to do, forever and ever."

"Well, I'm going to get some rest." Nathan got up and headed back into the house. He stopped, turned around, and walked back out of the veranda doors. "As far as the gun thing, you would've had to shoot Halle at least twice, possibly three times, and when she got back up she would've been pissed."

"Would it have given me a ten minute head start to safety?" Rube asked.

"Possibly. It depends as much on your adrenaline as Halle's. I don't know much about Glocks, they seem like powerful weapons. I know about being shot though."

"You've been shot before, Nathan?" The FBI Agent couldn't hide his surprise.

"To some, I am a monster." He replied. "There are times when I've lived up to the name. We haven't always lived in a civilized world."

"As quiet as it's kept, we don't live in a civilized world now."

"Right." The faintest glimmer of a smile passed over Nathan's very young and very serious face. "Goodnight, Agent Rubidoux."

"Goodnight."

Rube watched him walk away and knew it was time to get out of there. It had been a long day and between the confrontation with Halle, seeing Kath naked, and then finding out Jules was some kind of immortal oracle…he needed to be alone and work it all out. He wasn't going to find out any more about Paul Kirsch tonight or maybe ever. Just let this lead they were running down take him to the vampire so he could walk away clean. This was so over his head, Rube was struggling not to take in too much water and drown.

***

Just because she'd been walking in daylight for over a century didn't mean that Kathryn liked it. She did things to protect her skin, wore sunglasses and hats, but today there was a reprieve. The sky was grey, filled with dark clouds, and drenching rain. Kathryn was in Adams-Morgan; outside of a men's club called The Lion's Den. It wasn't open yet but her guest knew she was coming.

Taking a deep breath, she put her umbrella down and went in. Her eyes quickly adjusted to the minimal lighting; her fangs and nails extended to ward off potential danger. She scanned the large, empty room, her eyes found him occupying a table. Kathryn came and stood over him. He looked up before going back to his tortellini. A glass of red wine sat nearby.

"Don't hover." He said. "I've had so many women pissed at me over the years; I get nervous when a beautiful woman hovers."

Kathryn sat down, not taking her eyes off him.

"Are you thirsty?" He asked.

She made no effort to respond but he flagged the server anyway.

"Bring a glass of your finest for my companion."

The server nodded, stepping away.

"I think we have a friend in common, Kathryn."

"A friend who has no idea who and what you truly are, Senator Connelly." Kathryn replied, lighting a cigarette. "He didn't even stop to think how a nobody flat foot from The Bronx, no matter how clever, could become a Senator of one of the most powerful states in the Union. How long have you known Alexander Rubidoux?"

"A long time. Surely he doesn't know everything about me. It's better that way; for his safety. For what reason did you seek him out? Kathryn, you should've come to me."

The server returned with a goblet of blood but Kathryn didn't touch it.

"I didn't come to you because I don't trust you." Kathryn said. "I've never had a reason to."

"You'd trust a stranger instead?" Stephen countered. "A stranger from their world, who works for them and you just told him everything. What were you thinking? Paul would've…"

"You would do better right now to keep Paul's name out of your mouth. Alexander is nothing like them and I know that. You of all people will never get me to lose faith in the one thing I have left, which is my instinct. *You* work in their world; *you're* their golden boy."

"I look at it as keeping my friends close and my enemies closer."

"I don't believe anything you've ever said. You told Alexander that you don't know about Operation: Eternity and I know for damn sure that's a lie. You and Paul were keeping so many secrets."

"No more of a lie than the bullshit story he told me hoping I would take the bait. I love the guy but he's a lousy liar." Connelly sipped his wine.

"Where is Paul?" Kathryn asked. "I swear if he's harmed I won't stop until they're all on milk cartons. That includes the elusive Karen Pierson. My family has never done them any harm."

"I honestly have no idea about any of it."

"What kind of watcher are you? He is one of the most powerful men in our world; he sits on the Council. Someone should give a damn that he's gone. How far does this go and across how many worlds?"

"I only have two eyes, Kathryn. They've been observing some other things that you might find interesting."

"Don't keep me in suspense, Senator." Kathryn lifted the goblet and sipped. It was definitely some of the best; she drank a little more.

"Reapers are on the move." Stephen said.

"Where?" she asked. Expletives followed, barely under her breath.

"I'm not sure, but they've heard a rumor that Paul may be indisposed. The last information I received, about 12 hours ago,

Michael and Lex Marin were cutting their R & R on the Romanian countryside short and gathering their clan. Reapers don't leave vacation unless there's damn good reason."

"Who would tell them about Paul? I have sources too, Connelly, and it's still under wraps. I don't know for how much longer but it is today."

"A week is a long time in your world."

"How did you know he'd been missing a week?" Kathryn asked.

"I'm a watcher. I told you, you should've come to me."

Connelly's source had been vague and sketchy about Paul just as she had been about the Reapers. This even though he pumped her hard and paid her well. Good help was hard to find these days.

"Why should I take your word for anything? Why should I believe some unnamed source?"

"Because you have an adorable little girl with a squeaky voice who loves her Mommy and Daddy. You can't risk her head because you have serious trust issues."

"Don't you ever talk about my daughter." Kathryn's eyes flashed black and she showed her fangs. "If you're so damn altruistic, then tell me where her father is."

"I don't know, Kathryn. I'm not lying to you. Why would I let someone hurt one of the oldest people of your world? The things he's done are good, for all of us."

"Eternal human life is a good enough reason for some of you." She stood, tired of going in circles with him. She could rip his throat out right now she was so angry but the consequences of killing a watcher were heavy. Kathryn had enough to deal with. She put her cigarette out in his wineglass instead. "I'm a really busy woman. You'll have to excuse me, Senator."

"Rube is one of the best," Connelly's voice stopped her in her tracks. "That I will grant you. Still, he's hardly invincible. How do you feel putting his life at such great risk?"

"Don't concern yourself with how we get it done." Kathryn turned around. "Just know that we will."

"People in his own world would kill him for that amulet of immortality he's wearing around his neck. Does he even know the power he possesses?"

"Tell me the truth; they're going to kill Paul, aren't they? Tell me why this Pierson woman might come after him or if she's even involved. As far as I can tell she is a ghost, even by Langley standards. You seem to be the only connection, floating so effortlessly between our world and theirs."

"I would never do what you're accusing me of." Stephen replied. "I know you're frightened and upset but I've been there for you in the past, Kathryn. You'd do well not to forget that."

"Don't worry, Senator," She started toward the door. "My memory is quite long, thank you."

***

Rube and Kathryn met Dev and Jules at Absinthe later that evening. She hadn't discussed with him where she had gone earlier or who she had been with. Rube had a feeling that something was wrong. A part of him wanted to press her but he knew how close Kathryn was to breaking. Paul had been gone for seven days…the clock had all but run out. He prayed they were about to receive some good news.

"We're going to Kentucky." Jules said when they sat down.

Rube didn't like that he was sitting next to the Rottweiler but Morian seemed to pay him no mind. He was more relaxed than the first time the FBI agent saw him. A calm dog was a good dog.

"Whoa, Jules," Dev replied. "You're not going anywhere; especially to Kentucky."

"Why not? I can help."

"You've helped immensely, believe me. I'm not going to have an augur injured on my watch, and damn sure not you." He leaned and kissed her temple. "I checked the place out with Jules online and we'll definitely need reinforcements. No doubt the place will be locked down like Fort Knox."

"Who can we ask?" Kathryn asked. "I don't know anyone else I trust right now. I don't have any more favors." Max came by. He brought blood for Kathryn, lagers for Rube and Dev, and a fruity alcoholic beverage for Jules. Kathryn thanked him. "I've received information that the Marin clan is on the move. We have to get Paul back so he can help me protect our family. I can feel it; my children are in danger."

"Well, there are a few spirits who owe me a big favor." Dev said. He didn't want to use the marker, especially on a pro bono case for Kathryn the Great, but there were few other options now. He wasn't going to let the Kirsch family die if he could stop it.

"What situation could you have ever been in that spirits owe you a favor?" Jules asked.

"Do you remember Bosnia?"

"I try to forget it every day," Jules shuddered. "It was awful."

"Yeah it was but situations of that nature makes for strange bedfellows. I collected a few markers on that mission; gave some away too."

"What are spirits?" Rube asked as he drank his beer.

"Human beings have angels," Jules replied. "The supernatural world has spirits. They are 100% on the side of the light and totally badass, Boss. They're dead but not undead or ghosts."

"They've died in battle usually," Kathryn went on. "Or in committing some other selfless act. They are sent back to Earth to continue the battle in the name of the light."

"So they're warriors?" Rube asked.

"Not really," Kathryn shook her head. "In our world, warriors are rarely good guys. For this battle I think we could definitely use some spirits. Are you sure they'll help, Dev?"

"They owe me, and spirits don't shit on markers like some other people do. Not to mention Sam Kassmeyer has likely had a crush on you since The Crusades."

"I wasn't alive during The Crusades, smartass." She punched his arm. "You're going to reach out Sam?"

"I'll make some phone calls tonight…we'll get our reinforcements. We need to head out as soon as possible."

"I agree with that." Rube replied, biting back a yawn.

"Boss, I think you need to get some sleep. You'll need your strength over the next few days."

"I'm sorry I can't keep up with you guys. I'm trying my best."

"Alexander, you'll be no good lethargic and woozy." Kathryn replied, slipping her hand over his. "You're getting a good night's sleep; no arguments."

"You're doing better than I ever expected." Dev said. "You got some heart, Jack Ryan. You're not bad at all…for a human."

"I told you." Jules grinned. "Alexander Rubidoux is the absolute best human ever."

"Well the best human ever is exhausted. I'm gonna go and…" Rube stood but Kathryn took hold of his wrist. He tried not to tremble at her warm touch, sure that he failed. "What's the matter?"

"You can't go home."

"Why not?"

"It's too dangerous, Alex. The Reapers are surely on the move. I feel it inside of me and I don't want anything to happen to you. Since I can't feel your essence I need you to be close. Oh, and by the way, everyone you trust is not deserving of that trust."

"Am I supposed to know what that means?" He asked, trying to check his tone. Rube didn't want to sound peevish but could hardly see straight. It was past time for bed…two days past time.

"It means that you're with us until this is over." Kathryn said. "In every sense of the word."

Rube wanted to know where he was expected to go if he didn't go home.

"I like you, I guess, but I don't like you that much." Dev said. "Plus, Morian doesn't do new people."

The Rottweiler looked up when he heard his name. He looked at Rube as if he understood what his master said. His facial expression, if dogs had facial expressions, clearly said staying with them was out of the question. That was just fine with Rube.

"You're staying with me." Kathryn said. "We'll go back to your place, pack some things, and abandon it. It won't be forever; just for the time being."

"I don't like this, Kathryn. I didn't sign on to abandon my home, which sounds like forever by the way. It isn't much but it is mine."

Kathryn was sorry but her life was upside down as well. Charlie and Nathan were sharing a room while the girls slept with her. It was hard to shake up their lives but not tell them why. They missed their father and were losing all hope. She hated being deceptive with her children; hated that all this hard work might be in vain.

"We're going to get Paul back in a couple of days." Kathryn said. "You can forget you ever met me after that, I promise."

"Hey, that's not what I meant, Kath; you know that's not what I meant. I wouldn't say something like that." He sighed, squeezing her hand. He looked at Jules, who was content with her green drink. "Jules, am I going to see the other side of this?"

"Don't answer that, Jules!" Kathryn exclaimed. She looked at Rube with wide brown eyes. "How could you ask her such a thing? What are you thinking?"

Jules studied the both of them. She felt their pain and fear. She also felt their strength and growing connection. Her face remained sweet but neutral.

"The other side awaits us all," She said. "With open arms as a matter of fact."

"That answer sucks." Rube replied. "I could've gotten a better one from a Panda Express fortune cookie."

"Sorry, Boss, that's all I got."

"C'mon, Kath, we'll go to my place and get some stuff. I don't want you away from the children too much longer. Goodnight Dev; goodnight Jules."

"Goodnight."

Dev looked at Jules as Rube and Kathryn disappeared up the stairs to the exit.

"He isn't gonna make it, is he?"

"You gave him the amulet. He's safe as long as he wears it."

"That doesn't answer my question." Dev replied.

"Yes, it does."

000

They walked quietly through the drizzle to Rube's SUV. Kathryn was sick of the rain but kept any complaints to herself. She held onto Rube's arm while looking through the shadows they walked past. She felt the dread deep down; something would happen soon.

"Give me the keys, Alexander." She said.

"Huh?"

"Give me the keys." Kathryn held out her hand when they got to the car. "You're too exhausted to drive; I can do it."

"I guess it would be silly to ask if you have a license." He managed a smile.

"Wanna see it?" Kathryn asked.

"I trust you."

He gave her the keys and she opened the passenger side door for him. In the driver's seat, Kathryn pulled the seat up, started the ignition, and heard Brian Johnson singing *Back in Black*. It was a good song and managed to lift her spirits just a bit.

"Where am I going?" She asked, pulling out of the parking space. The car was huge, Kathryn was used to her Jaguar XJ8, but she wouldn't show Rube that she was out of her element.

"I live in Alexandria." Rube replied. "I'll give you the directions when we get there."

She nodded, heading for the freeway. The windshield wipers swishing back and forth made almost as much noise as the hard rock.

"I'm really sorry, Alexander."

"For what?"

"Dragging you into this. At the time I was too upset and maybe scared to think it through. If I would've, I would've realized they'd come after you. It was irresponsible. Both my side and yours is out for blood."

"My side?" Rube looked at her. "We're on the same side, Kathryn."

"I meant the government."

"Ah yes, the ones I trust who aren't trustworthy at all."

"I meant what I said."

"We've only known each other a week, but I most certainly know that." Rube replied. "You haven't minced any words since the coffee shop."

"I just feel guilty. Let me have it OK, it's an emotion I haven't experienced since…about three weeks ago."

That caught Rube off guard and he laughed. It was his real laugh and the sweetness of it made Kathryn laugh as well. She quickly turned solemn.

"Alexander, I'm serious."

"I know you are." He rubbed her arm but quickly pulled his hand back. "I appreciate it, but I'm being serious when I tell you to stop it."

"If you get injured, oh God, I don't want to think about something like that. But if something happens, you don't get a second chance."

"It's the life of an FBI agent." He said. "We risk our lives everyday on the side of justice. I don't mind…it's my calling."

"What about your family?" Kathryn asked.

"I don't have much of a family. That's the life of an FBI agent as well. But you do, and I'm going to make sure no one hurts them out of vengeance. I'm also going to make sure they get their father back."

"You're a good man, Alexander Rubidoux." Kathryn glanced at him before again focusing on the road.

"I'm just a man. We should all know the difference between right and wrong. You're going to pull off here."

Kathryn nodded, taking the exit. It was only a few more minutes before she was pulling into a parking space outside of a non-descript apartment complex. They got out of the car and walked into the building. After going up a short flight of stairs and through a heavy door, Kathryn stopped. She looked around, her fangs emerging from her gums.

Rube stopped as well, pulling his Glock from his hip. He knew something was off. Her game face, as Dev called it, didn't come out for nothing. They crept down the empty hallway to Apartment 204. The door was ajar.

"Get behind me, Kath." Rube said.

"Hey cowboy, I can probably fight what's in there better than you can." She replied.

"Right, OK, we're going in together on three."

Bursting into his place, Rube saw the living room and kitchen were in disarray. Something flashed by him and out the door.

"What the hell?" He didn't even have time to point his weapon.

Kathryn didn't get a chance to answer as another revealed himself and slapped her across the mouth. Bearing her fangs, she kicked the knife out of his hand. He grabbed her foot and threw her down on the floor. The whole thing was happening too fast for Rube…he didn't want to shoot the wrong person.

"Go after the other one!" Kathryn leapt up. "He'll slow down if he thinks he shook you."

"I don't want to leave you alone."

"Go," Kathryn managed to get a nice right hook in. "I'll be fine. Go, Alex!"

Rube turned, running out the door and down the hall. He was looking everywhere, not sure what might leap out at him. Knowing what he knew now, he wondered how many people behind these doors were of his world and how many of Kathryn's. It was scary thinking that something moved so fast, Rube wouldn't even see his death coming. He hoped that amulet around his neck was as protective as Kathryn made it out to be.

Out in the parking lot, Rube didn't see a thing. He checked behind cars and over by the dumpsters. Whatever it was, it was gone. He rushed back inside to make sure Kathryn was alright with the partner left behind. She was holding her own as he came through the doorway but the intruder pulled a second knife.

"Watch out!"

The thing slashed her near her collarbone before running out in a flash. Falling on the carpet, Kathryn's hand covered the wound as it bled profusely.

"Oh God, Kath."

"Help me. Get me something to stop the bleeding. Hurry!"

Nearly stumbling over what was once some halfway decent bar stools, Rube grabbed the roll of paper towel from the kitchen counter. He pulled nearly half of it off, quickly running it under the water, and helped Kathryn press it against the wound.

"What the hell were those guys?" He asked.

"They were lightning bugs. They're the…" Kathryn grimaced from the pain. "They're the dregs of our world; will do anything for money. Marin has to be behind this. No one respectable works with lightning bugs."

"Why are they called lightning bugs?"

"They have the ability to move with lightning speed but they also crawl in the dirt like bugs. There's a bug in your world with a glowing ass but they don't have anything to do with it." Kathryn folded the towel over to soak up more blood.

"That wound looks serious. I think we should go to the ER."

"I'll be fine; I just need to stop the bleeding. If I lose too much, I'll have to feed. C'mon," She let Rube help her up from the floor. "Grab a bag and let's get the hell out of here. They might come back with friends if they don't already have what they want."

Rube nodded. They made their way through the mess back to his bedroom. He ignored the disaster in there, grabbing a bag from the top of the closet. He wondered what they were looking for and if they found it. Kathryn sat down on the bed near the pillows.

"You said earlier that you didn't have family. Is that true, Alex?"

"Why?" He asked, going into the bathroom for toiletries.

"Because no one you love is safe anymore. Lightning bugs don't care who they hurt or kill. They're mercenaries and nothing is off limits. Money talks with these guys."

"My parents are dead. I have a brother in Seattle. I wouldn't call us estranged but I don't remember the last time I talked to him either. My ex lives in Silver Spring."

"Do you still love her?" Kathryn asked.

"What does that matter?" Rube's tone was defensive.

"It matters because they'll know and they will kill her. Breaking you is their agenda now."

"Alicia and I have been divorced for nearly a decade. She's remarried and has the children she said I could never give her. I'm sure if we saw each other on the street she would keep walking and I could live with that."

"Good," Kathryn nodded. "Well, what I mean to say…"

"I know what you mean, Kath."

"Alright. If you have any prized possessions, please bring them with you. I don't know when we'll be back."

Rube only took two things, the .45 Connelly gave him for his graduation from the Academy and the picture of his mother that he kept on the nightstand. She was holding her five year old son and they were both smiling. Rube never remembered being that happy as a child...it was the only proof he had that such a moment existed. He threw it in the bag, slinging it over his shoulder.

"How's the wound?" He asked.

"It hurts a little...I'll be alright. It'll close up soon even though it's pretty deep. I've been cut worse, believe me. Life hasn't always been the cosmopolitan streets of Washington, DC."

"Are you sure?"

They were out of the bedroom; Rube turned off lights as he went. He locked the door when they left, trying to shake the feeling that he'd never be back. Kathryn's words rang in his ear, breaking you is their agenda now. He couldn't wait to get Paul back. That would make this part worth it.

"I'm fine, Alexander, really." Kathryn replied.

"So you won't have to feed?"

"Probably not. I'll drink when I get home and...that really bothers you, doesn't it?"

"What?"

They were outside now. Kathryn wrapped the bloody paper towels with a towel she took from the apartment and dropped them in the dumpster. There was blood on her tank top and jacket but they were both dark colored so she would be alright until she got home. Kathryn and Rube climbed into the truck at the same time.

"Feeding?" Kathryn started the ignition.

"Of course it bothers me, Kathryn. The implication is to drain someone of their blood until they die. What if you accidentally brought someone over?"

"That can't be done by accident. It's a decision, made by two people and it bonds them for eternity. Feeding is feeding; bringing over is something else entirely. And by the way, life tip, we don't always feed to kill. It's complicated."

"I don't want to think about it." He said, shaking his head.

"It's who I am, Alexander. I can't change who I am. Even if I wanted to; nothing will ever change my instinct to survive. You have the same instinct…everyone does."

Rube didn't respond as they drove back into DC. It was a difficult conversation to have…he wasn't even sure if it was his place. He took a deep breath, trying to focus his mind on other things. There was enough to keep him occupied for some time to come.

CHAPTER 5

Kathryn stood out on the veranda, looking across the vast lawn into the dark night. This would be over soon, she could feel it, but who knew how it would end. The children were sound asleep, the house was quiet, and Kathryn could finally get a few moments to think. Now that she had it, she wished there was something else to think about. *With or Without You* on the radio helped, just barely.

"Kath..."

She jumped, turning to look at him with startled black eyes and her fangs out. In a matter of seconds, they went back to brown. Her fangs were slow to retract into her gums.

"I didn't mean to frighten you. I thought you might need this." Rube was holding her silk maroon robe. It matched the nightgown she was wearing; a nightgown Rube found quite attractive. He seemed to see right through it, her shapely body easy on the eyes, but it wasn't transparent. Just as it was in the bedroom, averting his gaze was almost impossible. He could at least try to look in her eyes. Right now he was being the worst kind of man.

"I like the night air, Alex, I'm fine. It's been quite a long time since anyone snuck up on me though."

"Why?" Rube asked.

"Why what, were you able to sneak up on me? I can't feel you."

"I've been hearing a lot in the last few days about feeling people. You gotta remember, I'm the human. I hardly know what you're talking about."

"I can't feel your essence because you're human." She almost smiled. *He was the human*; it was almost endearing if it wasn't utterly terrifying. "If you were of my world, I could. It's a defense mechanism." Kathryn took a clove from the table and lit it. "It's how we sense darkness, light, and everything in between."

"I've heard that before, about essence. Halle mentioned that she was having difficulty feeling her father. What about you, Kathryn? Can you still feel him? Is he...?"

"Paul is alive. If his essence were extinguished there's no way I wouldn't be aware of it. I've been wondering what it would even feel like."

"You two are quite close." Rube replied, sitting down at the small glass table. He wanted her to talk about him but didn't know how to ask. Some crackerjack FBI Agent he was. Maybe Rube just didn't want to hear how shitty Paul really was. He definitely didn't want Kathryn to have to lie like he wasn't.

"Have you ever known a couple that's been married for 50 or 60 years? Paul and I are like that, I guess. We're devoted parents to our children but haven't done much to nourish our own relationship in quite some time. But...it's complicated to say the least."

"Complicated is something I understand." Rube smirked and then cleared his throat. "Are you sure you don't want your robe, Kath? You're shivering; you might catch cold."

"I really appreciate that." She closed her eyes, exhaled, and smiled.

"Appreciate what?"

"That despite all of this, and it's a lot, you sometimes manage to forget that I'm not human like you."

Rube smiled too. When he thought about things like feeding or watched her change right before his eyes, it was quite clear who and what she was. Being a vampire wasn't the totality of Kathryn Spencer though. He couldn't pretend to know every facet to her. Her essence was vast. Rube knew that for sure even if he would never feel it. He knew it as well as he knew Bono's haunting lyrics to this song.

"Can you tell me what your definition of complicated is?" Rube asked.

"What?"

"Why is your relationship with Paul so complicated?"

"I've been an extension of Paul since he brought me over in the 1400s. We're blood of my blood but he's always at the controls. I hate to say that he owns me; the connotation makes me nauseous. But there have been times, in the not so distant past, when he acts as if he does. I'm more of a possession than a wife and surely not a partner.

"Our species lives by ancient rules; there are plenty who have changed with the times to survive and those who have not. He promised me something more but never quite…" Kathryn stopped. "Vampires aren't naturally monogamous you know, Agent Rubidoux."

"If the lore is to be believed, you like to sample as much flesh as you can."

"Something like that." Kathryn nodded. "We're familial, as I told you, blood is very important. It's not often that we choose life mates…why would we. The temptations of the flesh, even if you don't feed off of it, are quite powerful."

"Paul strays." Rube said. He shook his head and sighed. Who in their right mind would go to another woman's bed when this woman was waiting at home for him? Fighting or fucking, Kathryn Spencer was the kind of woman you wanted to experience it all with. Even at 1200 years old, men were still dumb. That wasn't a comforting thought.

"Stray is the wrong word."

"Is it?" he asked.

"Yes. I've been with others as well; it's not as simple as black and white. I don't know anything that is. Vampires desire flesh, in more ways than I can explain to you. Still, Paul is not an easy man to live with.

"We've had a lot of ups and downs over the centuries. It didn't help that we were both outcasts even before we became what we are. We've both had reasons to say fuck the world and everyone in it, including the people who might love us. I've left a few times but always returned.

"While my children are unable to walk in the day, their security is the most important thing to me. They weren't secure when I left the family. At least that's what I told myself. Maybe it's what Paul convinced me of…I hardly know anymore. You know the push and pull, you've been married."

"And now I'm divorced." Rube replied.

"Some of us don't have that option." Kathryn said. "You're supposed to be asleep, Alexander. I didn't bring you here to keep you awake with my stories. Jules was right; you need your strength for this trip."

"I felt a little weird in a large pink and white canopy bed." He replied. "Being surrounded by teddy bears and dolls freaked me out just a little bit. It's like that episode of *The Twilight Zone* when Telly Savalas…nevermind."

"I'm sorry about that, but Johanna's room adjoins mine so we can always reach each other. I feel safer with you right next door. While I can't feel you I know that you would hear if there was danger."

"Kathryn, there are other options; there have to be. I might sound like a sanctimonious jackass right now and be way out of my element but with all you're doing to bring Paul home I find it appalling that you're unhappy. He sounds like a cruel bastard from all I've heard."

"I'm thinking about my children." She said.

"I'm thinking about you." Rube countered.

"Thank you." Kathryn gave him a small smile. "I'm sure I've said this to myself more than once but at the moment there are other pressing issues."

"Do you really feel those Reapers coming?"

"I don't feel them in particular, I just sense darkness. Nothing is darker than reapers. It's a nagging feeling in the pit of my stomach and the base of my skull. I wish more than anything that it would go away. It makes me so nauseous. Maybe that's why I can't stop smoking…it almost settles my stomach."

"Could you have that feeling because Paul's in danger?" Rube asked.

"No," Kathryn sat across from him at the table. "That's another feeling altogether. I've experienced more emotions in this past week than I have in the past decade. That's sad and intriguing as hell at the same time. I was number than even I realized." She sighed. She didn't want to think about it anymore. "Would you tell me something, Alexander Rubidoux?"

"Yeah."

"What woman would be crazy enough to leave you? Your tenacity and dedication make you a keeper. The other things can be worked on…a lot of men are far more malleable than they think."

"What other things?" Rube raised an eyebrow.

"I can't name them offhand, we don't know each other that well yet, but all men have other things. Don't try to brush the first question under the rug." Kathryn lit another clove. She would stop smoking too when Paul came home. He hated it and had even forbade it on several occasions. Kath fought back and won, though the victory was symbolic with a side of pyrrhic. She did it mostly when she was out or when he wouldn't be around for a stretch. "How about a little reciprocity?"

"That dedication you talk about, it's to the Federal Bureau of Investigation." He took one of her cloves and lit it. The flavor was cherry vanilla; it was a funny feeling in his chest. "Kim and I met in graduate school and knew pretty early on that we would marry. When the Bureau recruited me, which we didn't see coming, she held on as long as she could. Then she let go. She wanted a husband, some children; a family. I promised her those things, in front of God, and I failed. She's better off without me."

"Do you truly believe that?" Kathryn asked as George Michael came through the speakers.

The song made her feel something else in her loins entirely. She stood, backing away from Rube, and leaned on the railing. The cool of the wrought iron helped the heat coursing through her bloodstream. Now was not the time for any of that but even after all this time, Kathryn couldn't always control her body. Lust had taken down more virtuous people than she. She was just grateful that she could still feel anything at all.

"Yes," Rube nodded. "I do. If we were still together she'd be in mortal danger because of my job. She's safe tonight in Silver Spring with the professor she married. I'm doing alright alone."

They didn't say much for a while. Kathryn just smoked and listened to the music. So many years, so many songs that read her like a book. She always wondered how songwriters did it. How did they dig into her guts, pull out her deepest feelings, and put them to melody? How dare they?

"I'm better off because of you, Alexander." She said. "I want you to know that."

"I'm just doing my job." Rube replied.

"You can say that, you can even mean it, but it's more to me." Kathryn practically whispered.

"Is it?"

"You've taken on a whole world; a world you didn't even know existed a week ago. I don't know if I could've done what you've done. I don't know how I'll ever be able to repay you. Most people I know don't do a damn thing for free."

"Getting that feeling out of the pit of your stomach will be enough thanks for me." He said, putting out the clove. Then he stood and held out his hand. "I need to sleep. Will you come with me?"

"You don't know how desperately I want to say yes."

"I didn't quite mean…" He dropped his hand, his cheeks flushing just a bit. When Rube smiled, a dimple poked into one of his cheeks. "OK, anything I say now will come out wrong and we'll go round and round like a bad Meg Ryan and Tom Hanks film. I really don't want to do that."

"If we go round and round, Agent Rubidoux, I insist that it's Cary Grant and Kate Hepburn all the way. Chemistry crackled between every line."

"I don't think I can do Cary Grant. Can anyone really do Cary Grant other than Cary Grant?"

"Alright fine, William Powell and Myrna Loy is my final offer." Kathryn replied.

"I'll save myself the embarrassment altogether and say goodnight now." Rube reached out for her hand again, and she met him halfway. When he squeezed it made his heart beat just a bit faster. He couldn't help but bring her hand to his lips, brushing gently across her knuckles. "Goodnight, Kathryn. Will you come up soon?"

"Yes," She nodded. "Goodnight."

He walked back into the house and through the dimly lit rooms. Rube did his best to ignore his heartbeat as he checked his pulse. It was moving a little too quickly as well. He needed to sleep. The next few days would be crucial.

They were heading to Kentucky and, come hell or high water, coming home with Paul Kirsch. Then, as Kathryn bluntly stated, he could forget he ever met her after that. When she said that, Rube got a nagging feeling in the pit of his stomach. He knew right then that he was in danger as well, and it had nothing to do with reapers.

***

The town of Hickman, Kentucky, population 1372, was about 12 miles outside of Fulton and the possible rescue of Paul Kirsch. Another two days had gone by; it was time to do this. Who knew what waited for them tomorrow but tonight there would be food, introductions, and a good night's sleep. Main Street was as jumping as it probably ever got in a town of this size.

Rube and Kathryn got out of their SUV. He saw Dev standing in front of Connie's Diner with two men and a woman. Then he watched Kathryn's whole expression change. Rube didn't know she was capable of such a smile. Her whole face took on a golden glow like nothing he'd ever seen before. It didn't seem possible for a woman to be as beautiful as she looked at that moment.

"Sam," She quickened her steps, rushing straight into the man's embrace.

He held her tight, wearing the smile of a content man.

"You're just as beautiful as I remember." He said, kissing the top of her head. "Time hasn't changed you at all."

"That's my curse." She replied, still holding on. "It's so good to see you; it's wonderful. I just wish it was under better circumstances."

"So do I. Why didn't you reach out to me, Kath?" Sam asked, taking her face into his hands. They were so close their noses touched.

"Well it's not like I could just look you up in the Yellow Pages. I haven't been thinking straight for this past week. Despite it all, you're not my guardian angel Sam, no matter how comforting that would be."

"Is the love fest over?" Dev asked. "The rest of us can wait inside if you two want to continue."

They both glared at him but Sam put some distance between he and Kathryn. He looked at Rube with a friendly grin.

"Alexander Rubidoux," Dev said. "These are spirits. That's Jacob Falconer, Sam Kassmeyer, and Mandy."

They looked like they were ready for a fight. Sam and Jacob were both Rube's height. Jacob was Native American, dressed in all black like Dev and wearing a long, brown trench coat. Sam had windswept brown hair and bright blue eyes. He looked comfortable in blue jeans, a black tee shirt, and a backpack slung over one shoulder. Amanda was small like Kathryn, about 5'6". She looked as if she'd been a cheerleader in high school, blonde and peppy. In khakis stuffed into combat boots and a white tank top, she now looked like she wrestled alligators.

"Just Mandy?" Rube asked as he shook their hands.

"Amanda North," The angelic faced woman replied. "Everyone calls me Mandy; I couldn't stop them if I tried."

Rube remembered that spirits had to die before returning to fight in the name of the light. She looked so young…he wondered what happened to her.

"Well, I'm Special Agent Alexander Rubidoux, the human. I prefer Rube."

"I told you I'd bring the reinforcements." Dev said, smiling. "You're looking at the biggest of the big guns."

"These big guns are hungry." Falconer replied. "Dinner is on you, Dev."

"Where's that adorable dog of yours?" Mandy asked as they went into the diner.

They were seated quickly and even though they didn't want to, they stood out. Sometimes there was nothing you could do about that. Six adults were sitting in a large booth, two of them black and one Native. All were dressed like road warriors. Not many of their kind inhabited this part of the state…they were strangers in a strange land. People would remember them but hopefully in 24 hours they would be on their way out of town.

"I had to leave Morian in the van and he's not happy. I promised to smuggle him out some pancakes."

They ordered two carafes of coffee while looking over the menu. Rube preferred tea and Kathryn didn't want anything. All she cared about was what they found at the facility.

"It's on the outskirts of Fulton," Falconer said in a low tone. "And it looks like a cakewalk. We watched it for the past two days and security is practically nonexistent."

"That cuz it's in the middle of nowhere." Dev added, pouring himself a cup of coffee.

"Inside I saw two security guards per floor in glass encased stations." Mandy said. "They looked bored."

"You got inside?" Rube asked incredulously. "How? Did you knock?"

"I can astral project, Agent Rubidoux. I was inside without being inside, you know?"

"I almost understood what you just said."

Mandy grinned as the waitress came over to take their order. Rube found out fighting in the name of light worked up an appetite. Spirits definitely liked to eat.

"Did you see Paul, Mandy?" Kathryn asked.

"I searched a lot of rooms but I didn't see him. I couldn't stay for long…it's quite a draining exercise."

"We're going in tomorrow." Sam said. "The security shift changes between two and two thirty so that's when we strike. Kath, you'll go inside with Mandy and Agent Rubidoux; you have 30 minutes to locate and rescue Paul. Any longer and the probability of fighting your way out goes up. We don't want to think about the firepower they may have."

"The second floor is where they keep patients." Mandy said. "The first floor and basement are medical facilities. Something hinky is definitely going on in there."

"They're not patients," Kathryn replied. "They're prisoners. I just hope Paul's there. If not, I'm out of options and hope. There is no more time. The Reapers…"

"No one will hurt you or your family." Sam reached for her hand. "Paul Kirsch has done his best to maintain peace and harmony as a leader in the Council. Unlike some of this brethren, he leads a relatively quiet existence and in no way exposes himself or our world. Let's just say we owe him one."

"You owe Marinescu one as well." Falconer said. "Remember New Jersey?"

"Of course I remember." Sam said through clenched teeth. He rarely let his anger get the best of him…younger spirits frequently followed Sam's shining example. But New Jersey had been horrific.

"What happened in New Jersey?" Rube asked.

"Long story short," Mandy put her hand on Sam's shoulder. "A pack of silverwolves were ambushed and murdered in Cherry Hill. The Boss sent Sam for their souls and that bastard Marin and his harlot got the jump on him. They were taking them to The Barrens but that wasn't where they belonged."

"Reapers are thieves," Sam picked the story up. "But I wasn't allowing it. Those wolves were good souls…one now battles in the light with us. I had to follow Marin and Lex for weeks. Bastards made me chase them to The Barrens; they treated it like a game." Sam shuddered. "I hate it down there but I had a job to do. I got those souls back but yeah, I owe Marin. Still, that's not the only reason I'm doing this."

Sam looked at Kathryn and she smiled at him. Rube looked at them looking at each other and wondered which aspect of the long story short that was.

***

"Did something happen between you and Sam Kassmeyer?" He asked.

They were back at the tiny motel in Hickman. Kathryn sat on the bed drinking a goblet of blood. She'd just called home to check on her family. Jules and her girlfriend Bashira, were watching over the children. Jacob Falconer sent another spirit, Matthew Weaver, to keep an eye on them as well. He would be spending the night.

"I'm sorry, Alex, what?" Kathryn came out of her thoughts, giving him her full attention. This was almost over, she hoped, and she could stop worrying constantly about her children's safety.

"Did something happen between you and Sam Kassmeyer?" He repeated.

"What do you mean?"

"Were you two lovers? Hell, are spirits even allowed to have lovers?"

"Spirits are kinda like Jedi," Kathryn replied. "They are encouraged to leave all of that behind to battle in the name of the light. Temptations of the flesh are mostly frowned upon."

"But…" Rube pressed.

"Love is the strongest of all emotions. No one knows that better than the light. The Boss compromises."

"Who is The Boss?"

"He's just The Boss." Kathryn said with a shrug. "I'm gray Alex, soulless, so I will never walk in the light but am capable of not embracing the darkness. It's all pretty complicated, as these things are."

"What happened with Sam, Kathryn?"

"He saved our lives…it's what spirits do."

"Our?"

"My entire family." Kathryn said.

"When? How did he do that?"

"You know what," she held up her hand. "I'm not on the witness stand or in an interrogation room. You might want to check your tone. I've been revealing a lot about myself, which is not easy for me. I don't know a damn thing about you. Everything I've been through is not for you to know, process, and scrutinize. Jesus, Alexander."

Rube took a deep breath. He'd gone too far; certainly didn't mean to interrogate her. He was under a lot of stress, worried about tomorrow's mission, but he wouldn't take that out on Kathryn. They were in this together. He could ask but if she didn't answer then he wouldn't press. It had probably been hell for her just to give him what she already had.

"How do you say jackass in Russian?" He asked, sitting beside her on the bed.

"There's no translation for that, unfortunately." She replied.

"I'm sorry about my tone, Kath. You're right; I have no right to interrogate you. Even more than that, I don't want to. You've told me enough already."

"That's right, I have, and I know nothing about you. Well, I know about your apartment…your apartment had divorced guy written all over it."

"Why not single guy?" Rube asked.

"Because single guys are trying to impress women enough to get laid," Kathryn replied. "That place didn't impress anyone."

"Hey, in my defense, you only saw it after it was trashed."

"Oh," She smirked. "OK."

"I'll make you a promise." He said trying not to grin. "When this is all over I'm going to buy you dinner and tell you my story. I gotta warn you though, it's short and boring. I'm going to tell you anyway."

"Short is fine because I don't often eat much."

Rube smiled. He put his hand on her shoulder, asking if she was OK. Kathryn nodded.

"Sam smuggled my family out of Poland." She said.

"When?"

"1944."

"Oh my God, Paul's Jewish."

"Yes, and I'm Black Russian. That's an actual term and group of people, Alexander." Kathryn said. "Everything isn't always about Paul though using this particular story to express that is a bad example. Things had passed uncomfortable years before and had quickly escalated to deadly as the Allies turned the tides. We were in hiding and knew time wasn't on our side. After the Blitzkrieg, Poland was cut off…we lost nearly all connection with the outside world. Somehow Sam found us and got us out. He took Paul, Halle, and Charlie first to America. By the time he came back for Nathan, Johanna, and I, I truly believed we would die there.

"The Red Army was advancing. People were getting on trains and never coming back. They were emptying out the ghettoes as fast as they could when they knew all was lost. The Final Solution…three words for such a monstrosity. It was worse than anything I'd ever seen in Russia and I lived through the pogroms, Alex, and the Bolshevik Revolution. No place was safe because the whole continent was at war. It took almost two weeks to get out; we were in the middle of the Warsaw Uprising.

"I cannot imagine the risks Sam took to rescue us. Reapers were everywhere; it was a party for them. They were snatching the souls of the dead and helping others along. He got us out though, protected us like we were his own family. Johanna was just a baby; she was frightened and he was good with her. He eased her fears, told her that he would always look after her. She's called Sam her guardian angel ever since. I still don't know how he found us but we'd be dead if he wouldn't have."

"I thought there were only two ways to kill a vampire." Rube replied.

"If the Reapers hadn't found us and handled that, surely we would have wished for death by the time it was over. Alex, I don't know what I'm going to do if we don't find Paul tomorrow. I want this to be over."

"We've come this far and we're going to finish it. And I'm sure I don't need to tell you, but you can stand on your own two feet without Paul. I've watched you do it…it's all I know of you. But I'm also going to fight like hell to get him back to his children."

"That's exactly why I'm doing this, for my children. Whatever happens after I need them to know I brought their father back to them because I love them and they love him."

"We'll get him." Rube rubbed her shoulder. "We've got reinforcements." He smiled and was happy when Kathryn did the same. Rube cleared his throat. "So, you and Sam never…"

"No Alexander," Kathryn shook her head. "We have not. What the hell does that matter? Would you like me to make you a list of all my past lovers for the FBI database? It might take a while."

"No, of course not. None of that matters." he didn't say anything else. What right did he have to know those kinds of things about Kathryn? It wasn't her fault that he couldn't get the vision of her and the handsome spirit locked in a passionate embrace out of his mind. Rube needed to focus, and not on that. There were more important things on the line right now.

"I need a smoke." She stood up. "I'll be right back."

"Oh no, we're going together. That's how we roll until this is over, remember? You enforced the rule."

"How we roll? You don't look like you roll, Agent Rubidoux."

"You should know by now that looks can be deceiving, Ms. Spencer."

"Touché. Well, c'mon then, let's roll." Kathryn made a face and Rube smiled. She took his hand, pulling him toward the door. There was little reason for joy but they had to hold onto something. They held onto each other.

CHAPTER 6

Kathryn walked out onto the motel room porch and was surprised she wasn't alone. It was who the fuck knows o'clock, but Sam Kassmeyer was sitting on the bannister. He was facing out as if he would jump but Kath knew that he wouldn't. He was shirtless, barefoot, and wore Wrangler jeans. She took a moment to admire his physique. In the shadows of the dim porch light there were expansive wings that mesmerized her. She'd seen them once, with her own eyes; what an experience that had been.

"What are you doing out here?" she asked, lighting a clove.

"Talking." Sam replied, glancing back at her.

"Talking to whom?"

"The Boss."

"Does she ever answer back?"

"You're being facetious." Sam smiled a bit.

"I am." Kath nodded. She sighed and looked out into the night. The sky in DC had nothing on Kentucky. It was full of stars, bright and bold. The moon, a little more than a quarter, sat low in the distance. It was absolutely beautiful. If there was a God, here would be the perfect place to commune with her.

"It's been so many years but I can't get Johanna to stop saying that prayer." Kath said.

"Which prayer?"

"Now I lay me down to sleep. It's a ritual and she doesn't miss a night. Except she always says 'if I should die before I wake, Guardian Angel Sam better come and get me. Amen.'"

"I may have taught her that part." Sam grinned.

"Clearly."

"Has Agent Alexander Rubidoux been able to help you in a way no one else could?"

"I don't understand the question."

"I was surprised when Dev said the FBI was working on this case. They're...very public."

"Alexander is a kidnapping specialist, so that was part of it." Kath said. "People disappear and he finds them with a high success rate. I also knew that Paul had dealings with certain subsections of the government and I was concerned they were behind his disappearance. Who better to spy on the government than the government?"

"And you trust him?"

"He got us all the way to Kentucky. And I don't mean that he drove the car, Sam."

The spirit nodded.

"I am so sorry this is happening to you and your family, Kathryn. Are the children alright?"

"Johanna doesn't know what's happening. Nathan is frightened and Halle is angry with everyone. It's overwhelming. All of it is incredibly overwhelming."

"What do you need?" Sam asked, reaching back to take her hand in his. He laced their fingers, squeezed, and Kathryn exhaled. It came out like a moan of ecstasy that made her quiver.

"Peace of mind." She took a deep inhale, felt as if she could barely breathe. "Strength."

"You've got strength by the ton and have harnessed it for centuries."

"Focus."

"What do you want to focus on?"

"Making things better for myself and my children. All of this fear and rage inside of them is surely a manifestation of my being trapped in a cage for over a half century. I tried so hard to make things bearable for them. I tried so hard to make sure they didn't hate their father."

"They don't." Sam shook his head.

"I have to leave him, Sam. I want to find Paul, alive. I want him to be alright for himself and for our family. But I can no longer be his mate. I have to be far away from him. I'm tired of feeling dead inside but still being forced to live every day. This week reminded me that there are other emotions and even when feeling them tears you completely apart inside, that's its own kind of magic."

"Is there someone else?"

Sam couldn't advocate infidelity. He couldn't as the man he once was or the spirit he'd become almost too long ago to remember. Kathryn was going to do what she wanted, they all had free will. He was hoping to find out what that was before giving his two cents.

"There has been in the past." She replied.

"And now?"

"Now there's only me, Sam. For the first time in probably a century that's good enough. I've lost me and I need to get her back. If I'm going to live forever I don't want to be unhappy anymore while doing it."

"Whatever you need from me," he held her hand to his lips. "Just ask. Call me Kath; I always hear you."

"Why are you so good to me?" Kath asked. She knew what spirits were and what they did. They were a force for light and good…that was surely needed in their world. As special as they were, Sam was something even more special.

"Because I love you." Sam let go of her hand and spun around on the bannister. "I have faith in all you've done over the years and will continue to do. You are a precious gift, Kathryn, and we're connected in so very many ways."

"Even though I have no soul?"

"We all have afflictions."

"You don't."

"Oh yes," Sam laughed. "I do. None of us are perfect, we just do our best to walk the path closest to the light. As long as there is breath in your body, you can do that. But right now you should rest. Tomorrow is a big day."

"I'm going to have a clove. I didn't quite enjoy the first one." She looked down at the half-smoked clove by her feet. The force of Sam's touch made her drop it.

"Well, sweet dreams." he leaned and kissed her temple.

"Thank you Sam; goodnight."

Alone on the porch, Kath lit another clove. There was a warm breeze blowing through the trees. The temperatures had fallen but it was barely cool. She'd tried for a few hours to sleep; hadn't been successful. Despite it all, Kathryn was still a night dweller.

It was her nature as a vampire and very hard to change. So much had changed since the dawn of the 20th century. In a little over 100 years more changes had come than in her first four centuries as a vampire. People just weren't meant to live this long. But here Kathryn was and she wanted to be happy. It seemed fantastical, sometimes improbable, but she wanted it anyway.

With one last puff, she flicked away the clove and went back into the motel room. Alexander was in his bed. He was sound asleep; looked at peace. For a while she just looked at him and then sat down on the edge of the bed. His bare chest rose and fell with his sleeping.

Kath sighed, placing her hand over his heartbeat. The strength of it made her never want to let go. Suddenly, Alexander seized her wrist and his eyes flew open. He looked at her with wide blue eyes that slowly started to calm.

"Kathryn? Kath?" he sat up some, loosening his grip on her wrist but still holding on. "What are you doing?"

"It looked as if you weren't breathing." She lied. "I was double checking. You're not getting off that easy."

"I'm alive."

"I see that now." Kathryn almost smiled. She flexed her fingers. "Wanna let go?"

"Huh?" Rube looked down at her hand. "Oh, right, I'm sorry. I thought you were going to kill me. Well, I thought that before I realized you were you."

"Go back to sleep, Alexander." She patted his chest and got up from the bed. "No one is going to kill you."

"Do you need anything?" he asked.

"No."

"You don't sound alright."

"I'm fine, just ready for morning to come and this to end. Goodnight."

"Goodnight."

He watched her climb into the bed next to his but wondered if she would sleep. He didn't know how much sleep a vampire really needed to function and she surely wasn't in the mood for another lesson right now. There was a heavy tension in the room; Alexander wasn't sure if it was his sleepiness or something real. But he was sure that Kathryn needed time to get her thoughts and emotions together about what might happen tomorrow. For once, since all of this started, he wasn't going to insist on being privy to the routine.

***

The next day was hot, dry, and sunny. They parked Rube's SUV and Dev's black van off the highway and walked a mile down a dirt road to the facility. No one was around; if it were a movie there would've been tumbleweeds. Kathryn hated it already. She wore khakis, a green tank top, and a baseball cap. Sunglasses covered her eyes and SPF 75 was on her exposed skin. Still, it was nearly unbearable.

"Are you alright?" Sam asked. Both he and Rube were walking beside her. "Are you wearing enough protection? Did you have enough blood this morning?"

"I'm fine," She stroked his arm. "Thanks. How the hell is Falconer wearing a trench coat? I'm roasting just looking at him."

"We're the same temperature all the time." Falconer said from a few feet ahead. "Changes in weather have no effect on us."

"That must be nice." Rube replied.

"It has its perks." Sam said. "We travel everywhere from sub-Sahara Africa to Siberia, Agent Rubidoux, at a moment's notice. We rarely have time to pack."

"This should be easy." Falconer said. "We've planned for almost every scenario."

They were about 100 feet away now, crouched in the bushes and brush. Rube wished someone would've mentioned this part…the bugs were going to eat him alive.

"Sam, Dev, and I will keep watch while you, Rube, and Mandy go in and get Paul. There should be few obstacles in your way."

"Should be." Rube mumbled. "How do we get in without setting off alarms? I can't astral project."

"There's a first floor window in the back that leads to a janitor's closet." Mandy replied. "The back stairs are next to it so we'll take them up to the second floor. From what I could tell, back stairwells are not alarmed or keyed."

"If the Acme Patrol shows up, we got your back." Dev said. "I don't see this turning into the OK Corral but you never know. If they have guns, so do we."

"Getting into the gate will be the most difficult part." Sam said.

"I got it all covered." Mandy pulled wire cutters and a box of stick matches from her cargo pants pocket. She was grinning as if she just discovered electricity. "This is known in layman's terms as a diversion."

"The Boss is not going to be happy about fire." Falconer said.

"There are exceptions to every rule…this is it." Mandy replied. "It's important, Jacob."

The Apache nodded. This was a 'do what you gotta do' mission. Still, he would have to explain their actions to The Boss. Being team leader wasn't all shits and giggles.

"Why doesn't The Boss like fire?" Rube asked. He couldn't help it, but every time he said that he thought of the spirits having to answer to Bruce Springsteen. Surely there were worse people to think of as God. "In ancient times it was seen as a cleansing method."

"This isn't ancient times, Agent Rubidoux," Sam replied. "It's very destructive and nearly impossible to control. But Mandy is right, this is important. We have to do this now; it's too hot out here for Kathryn."

"Perhaps you should've stayed back at the motel." Rube said. He looked at her and Kathryn looked nauseous. The sun beamed down on them.

"To hell with that, Alex. This is my battle and I refuse to sit in a motel room while the big bad men fight for me and my family. Let's do this before I fry…a vampire with a tan is not pretty."

"Go," Falconer instructed. "Thirty minutes, Mandy, no more."

They nodded and set off. Mandy went to the side of the building, setting a small fire in the dry brush. It quickly grew. As four security guards rushed toward it, she ran back to the other side. Cutting the gate, the three of them climbed through. They rushed to the back window, Rube hoisting Mandy up to open it.

Once she climbed in, she reached out for him. Kathryn hoisted him up, her strength boggling his mind. Then she jumped up and through the window. The room was pitch black so Rube turned on his pocket flashlight. He and Mandy gave Kathryn a few moments to recover from the harsh exposure to direct sunlight. She leaned on the cool cinder block walls and took deep breaths. She took off her glasses, placing them on the shelf by some cleaning products. Mandy peeked out the door; saw an empty hallway.

"It's time to go guys, now."

The side stairwell wasn't alarmed and the three made their way up to the second floor. No one intercepted them. This time Rube peeked out the door. The hallway was again empty. He saw eight large, white doors, four on each side. The hallways then went in two directions at the end, no doubt to more doors.

"I think this might take more than a half hour." He said, sighing. "It could be countless doors."

"I'll just slip into each one and see if he's there." Mandy replied. "Normally I could do it from here but this place is too much of a maze. I need to be closer to the source. You two wait here so you won't be out in the open. That'll be a good way for us to get caught."

"I don't like how quiet it is around here." Kathryn said. "It's like the calm before the storm."

"Don't worry, it's in and out. Kathryn, I'll send you a sign when I find him."

"Right." She nodded as Mandy disappeared.

"What kind of sign will she send if we can't see her?" Rube asked. He didn't like just standing in the stairwell like this. Anyone could just walk up or down, find them, and shoot them. He took his gun from the holster. Always be prepared, something he'd never quite been on this job.

"We'll feel each other. If she finds Paul, I'll know."

"Oh right, you can feel her essence as well."

"Yes," She nodded. "We all sense the light and the darkness around us."

Rube nodded and then they just stood there quietly. It was awkward but he said nothing. They were so close to solving this; a little awkward silence was bearable.

"What?"

"Oh my God, Alex," Kathryn grabbed his hand. "He's here. He's here and Mandy found him. Let's go."

They snuck out of the stairwell. Rube had to stop her from running up the hallway like a madwoman. It was still dangerous territory; they had to take their time. He didn't like how quiet it was either. Had the government decided to take a Saturday off?

"He's in there." Mandy pointed to a white metal door with no window.

"Is he...?" Kathryn could hardly finish her sentence. She felt so cold; something was wrong.

"There is life force in him." Mandy replied. "The door's bolted though."

Kathryn turned the knob...she practically tore the door off the hinges. She rushed in, her two companions behind her. The room was made to look like a traditional sitting room, with plush chairs and book-filled shelves, but it was nothing more than a prison. Paul was in an easy chair sleeping. He looked ashen, older, and a book of Whitman poems lay across his lap. Kathryn gasped, falling on her knees in front of him.

"Pasha," She touched his face. "Wake up, luybov[i]...please."

"Katya," He opened his eyes and saw her. "Moya[ii] luybov. Don't let me wake up from this dream."

"It's not a dream. We're here to take you home. C'mon, we have to go."

"Don't go." He held her hand.

"We're going...together." Kathryn replied. "I'm really here; this is real."

"Katya," Still weak, Paul seemed to come alive. "Katya, moya luybov. Plot ot ploti[iii]; krov ot krovi[iv]. Navsegda[v],"

"Navsegda; Plot ot ploti, krov ot krovi." She kissed both his cheeks. He was so clammy. "Come, we're getting out of here."

"I don't have the strength." He said as she pulled him up from the chair.

"I'll carry you all the way home on my back if I had to."

Rube heard a noise and looked behind him.

"Shit, we've got company. We have to go, Kath, now!"

She nodded, throwing Paul over her shoulder as if he weighed no more than a knapsack. They ran out of the room, security on their tail yelling for them to stop.

"Freeze or I'll shoot."

Gunshots rang out and Rube fired back. He ducked behind a wall as bullets came in his direction. Mandy, who seemed to be running right into the gunfire like a madwoman, threw Chinese stars that stabbed the guards. Rube used the lull in gunfire to fire more shots as they backed down the hallway. Some guards were still close behind.

"Go, Kathryn…run!"

She did, rushing into the stairwell. Gunfire crackled behind her. She practically flew down the stairs and back into the closet. Kathryn grabbed her glasses, careful jumping out of the window. She made sure to land on her feet, which wasn't the easiest thing she'd ever done. Outside, her eyes darted back and forth but she didn't see anyone. As she pulled Paul through the gate, Dev's van pulled up. Sam opened the back sliding door.

"Get in." He said.

"I have to go back for Alex and Mandy. They were shooting their way out. Take him."

Sam did as she asked, carefully laying Paul on blankets in the back. Kathryn was already halfway back to the building when Mandy and Rube tumbled out the window. He was limping from a bad tuck and roll. They ran toward her; Kathryn saw the blood.

"Oh my God, are you alright?" She asked Rube as Mandy jumped in the van.

"It's just a graze; I'm fine. I'm wearing Kevlar."

"You can't get in the van. Paul will smell the blood…he might try to attack."

"We gotta go." Falconer yelled from the front seat. "Let's move, folks."

"Go. We'll run back. Go, Dev!"

The van took off and so did Rube and Kathryn, on foot. No one was following them, a good sign but both thought it had been a little too easy to sneak and break someone out of a government facility. And a secret government facility at that. Where were the tanks, copters, and snipers? What the hell was going on?

"Are you sure you're alright?" She asked mid-stride. The sun was brutal at this hour.

"I'm more concerned about you and this sun." Rube replied. "It really is just a nick. Thanks for the warning about getting in the van though."

"He's really weak; he needs to feed or he'll die. I guess I should tell you the third way to kill a vampire. You can deprive them of blood. It'll take about 72 to 96 hours to kill them, like depriving a human of water. I think the reason there wasn't more insanity back there is that they're done with what they were doing…Paul was of no more use to them."

"Well there's plenty of blood back at the motel."

"Not drink, Alex, Paul needs to feed. Love it or hate it; it has to be done."

"What do you plan to do about it?" Rube asked. "You can't just pluck someone off the street."

"No." Kathryn shook her head. "I'll feed him."

"What? You'll…"

"It's not as bad as it sounds."

"I'm not sure that I believe you."

"C'mon, we're almost there. Run a little faster, slowpoke."

"Slowpoke? I got grazed with hot lead, woman, before tumbling out of a damn window. I took a bullet for you."

"Excuses, excuses, Rubidoux. Move your ass."

He couldn't help but smile as he quickened his pace back to their getaway car. They got to the fork in the road, hopped in, and Kathryn sped off toward Fulton.

***

She sat on the edge of the bed, taking Paul's face in her hands. Rube stood at the motel room door and watched. He'd pulled all the shades and curtains…his eyes were still adjusting to the darkness. She ran her lips over Paul's clammy forehead before looking at Rube.

"You don't have to stay for this." She said. "It might not be pretty."

"I'm not leaving you...that was the deal."

She nodded, turning back to Paul. Kathryn couldn't explain why she felt uncomfortable having both men in the room. It didn't matter; there were more important things to worry about now.

"Open your eyes, Pasha[vi]; I need you to look at me."

"They're trying to create everlasting life, Katya." Paul's hand caressed hers. "They're playing God and in some ways I helped."

"What else is new? I think you got in over your head with whatever this is, not that you'd ever think you did. You never expected anyone to turn on you though their plan was perfect. Did Stef Connelly set you up?"

Rube was surprised to hear his old friend's name but he didn't show it. The Senator, the vampire, and possibly the CIA...he should've known. It was hard to get to the top without harboring your share of secrets and collecting political markers.

"I don't know, I don't know love; he wouldn't do that to me. We've been through a lot together. I was trying to keep this from getting more out of control than it already was."

"Alright, don't talk about it anymore. You're really weak and you've got to feed."

"I don't like male flesh." Paul slowly turned his head toward Rube. "You know that."

"Yes I do, but he is not your treat. I am."

"Absolutely not," He was adamant even in his weakness. "No."

"You feed or you die, Paul. Just a little, not too much." Kathryn held out her wrist.

"Katya…"

"Don't you dare argue at a time like this. You want to die for some machismo? How long have they been depriving you?"

"I'm not sure. It was hard to keep track of days and nights in a room with no windows. I don't want to hurt you. I made promises not to hurt you."

"I'm a big girl," She replied knowing that he'd hurt her a thousand times before. "I didn't come this far to lose you now. Your children would never forgive me and Alexander here might kick my ass. Take my wrist."

"I promise not to hurt you." He took her wrist and gently kissed it. His fangs came out and he bit into the skin.

Kathryn winced, whimpered, but made no other sound. Paul was ravenous though he stopped before he had his fill.

"More; you need it." Kathryn pushed it toward his mouth.

"You need it as well."

"You must."

"No," his voice got deep and dark. "No more."

Rube rushed to the bathroom and grabbed a towel for the wound. He remembered how quickly she could bleed from the fight with the lightning bugs in his apartment. He handed it to her.

"Thank you, Alex."

Paul smelled the blood on his shirt. He sat straight up, fangs out, and eyes completely black. They flashed brimstone. His face could only be described as monstrous. Rube let out a shout of surprise, stumbling back and falling on his ass. Kathryn put a gentle hand on Paul's chest. He was too weak to attack. The show of force was just that, a show.

"Alexander, you have to go now. Falconer should look at your wound and patch it up. You also need to change your shirt."

"Are you two alright?" He asked. "Are you alright?"

"I should be asking you that. You've taken more than a few knocks today. We're fine and I'll heal. Go next door, get checked out, and I'll feel even better."

Rube nodded. Picking himself up from the carpet, he shook off his sore hip. He reached out for Kathryn but balled his hand into a fist before reluctantly leaving the room. Watching him go, she turned and stroked Paul's face. He would probably need to feed again but a drink in between would be good for him. She wrapped the hand towel around her injured wrist, went to the bathroom for the tumbler, and then to the mini-fridge for some blood.

000

"How is he?" Rube approached Kathryn as she smoked a clove on the balcony.

"He's asleep. He'll probably sleep all the way home. The feeding helped but he'll need more. I'll get him some as soon as we get to DC."

"Was he able to tell you what happened to him?"

"No. I don't know if he ever will, but I've been putting two and two together for days now. Paul had to be involved in that operation, Alex. How else would he ever let someone get that close to him without tearing them to shreds? I know he has friends at Langley. Your friend knew it too. That's what's most important to me."

"We'll be leaving in a few hours." Rube said, trying to take in all she'd said. The man could be responsible for the disappearance and death of hundreds of his own people. How much money was that worth these days? "Falconer thought it would be good to go at dusk."

"I agree," Kathryn replied, plucking the clove over the railing. "I need to get Paul home where he can recuperate fully. Seeing the children will be good for him…for them as well. I need to thank you for everything you've done."

"No you don't." Rube shook his head. "When I agreed to it, I knew it would be a dangerous mission."

"You kinda took a bullet for me, Alexander. I joked about it earlier but that's not funny."

"I did what was needed to reunite a family. It's my job as an FBI agent and I take that seriously. Besides, I wasn't hurt. Maybe there is some power behind this amulet you won't let me take off."

"More than you realize." Kathryn said. "I'm going to thank you anyway, whether you think I should or not. If I were you, I would've turned me down."

Rube didn't believe that and he told her so.

"Paul didn't deserve what happened to him."

"They're all savages," Kathryn's eyes turned black. "They'll pay for the sins they committed but not at my hand. I am so sick of vendettas and vengeance. I think that's why it was so easy in the beginning for me to close the curtains and pretend none of it existed. Feeling like a second class citizen here didn't help. Some days I feel as if I've lived too damn long but nothing has changed. It's only getting worse."

Why do you think Stephen Connelly would set Paul up?" Rube asked.

"He's a Watcher; they watch over our world and yours. They fix things, negotiate, keep profiles low; that sort of thing. He is the major link between Paul and the federal government that doesn't involve Paul's financial work. As far as I know, Operation: Eternity has always been on his radar. I've never really trusted him but still have a hard time believing he had a direct hand in Paul's kidnapping.

"Connelly isn't perfect...they likely trusted the wrong people and Paul paid for it. He and Paul were into something together that got out of control. That's a real possibility. Or maybe I'm just being naïve as hell about the entire thing because the alternative is horrible. Watchers are supposed to be peacekeepers, first and foremost. Conflict in our world would only bring more drama to theirs. It would threaten to expose them and everything else. Connelly's been around a long time...he knows how to cover his ass and his assets."

"Is Steph immortal?" Rube asked. "Is he...something else?"

"Watchers are always human; they have to be for what they do. I wouldn't wish walking the fine line between our two worlds on the strongest of souls."

"I've known Stephen Connelly for over a decade." Rube said.

"I know that." Kathryn nodded.

"How?"

"He told me. I don't know the details, Alexander, and don't very much care to be honest. This part is over; I can't worry about him now. I need to get home to my children. That feeling hasn't left the pit of my stomach."

"Did you call home?"

"I spoke with Jules and she told me that all's quiet. Of course all was quiet in that building today when security showed up without warning. Marin is coming, Alex...I can feel it. I need to be ready when he gets here."

"We'll be ready." Rube replied.

"You've done enough; you owe me nothing. Seriously, you've already put your life in enough jeopardy. Without you, I never would've found Paul. I don't want anything to happen to you. I carry 500 years of guilt and regret. I can't carry that. It's time to exit stage left."

"I don't plan on exiting until this is finished. Anyway, they're after me now. This Marin character doesn't sound like the type to let me go on my merry way because I'm back at my desk in DC. I've seen and know too much. I have to see it through to the end."

Kathryn nodded but didn't respond. She just took a deep breath, lighting another clove. She reached down and slipped her hand in his. She felt so disconnected; needed to feel connected to something. She needed to feel connected to him.

Paul was lying in that bed and she didn't feel the joy she thought she would. There was just emptiness...why was there just emptiness? When he laced his fingers through hers, Rube's breath caught in his throat. Her heat drew him in and without his consent, Rube's lips brushed across her hairline. Kathryn moaned softly and leaned into him. Rube wrapped his other arm around her back; he was finally holding her. His lips were still on her skin.

"Hey, you...oh." Mandy cleared her throat.

They came apart completely. Kathryn looked at her as Rube sighed. He stuffed his hands in his pocket and took a step away for good measure. That was close; that was too damn close.

"Falconer says we're setting off in about an hour."

"Thanks, Mandy." Kathryn replied.

"Sure." She didn't linger, going back into the room she shared with Jacob and Sam.

"I should..." Rube was at a loss for what to say now that they were alone again. He'd crossed the line. He needed to turn around and plant his feet firmly on the other side. Bad things happened when cases became personal. But he couldn't move and suddenly his arms felt so empty.

"I need to check on Paul." Kathryn used one clove to light another. "I haven't smoked this much since Poland."

"Saying this past week and some change has been stressful is an understatement." Rube said.

"I try not to expose the children to my bad habits. I was doing really well for a while. They can be hellions sometimes; they don't need me adding fuel to the fire."

"You're a wonderful mother to all of them. Your sheer will kept your family together through this crisis."

"I love my children, Alexander."

"I know that." He'd seen that love first hand. Tough, firm, caring, sweet, and at times even docile; Kathryn Spencer had a hell of a lot on his own mother and her heart didn't even beat. Did it?

"For the past 300 some years, through hell and back, Paul and I have vowed to love and protect our family. It's a vow I've never broken."

Rube understood that; it was what parents were supposed to do. He couldn't imagine the fear she felt in thinking something terrible could happen to them. He wanted to reach out to her, feel her again, and be felt by her. They were still in danger...even he felt that now.

Rube didn't know a Reaper from a Rottweiler. He wasn't sure what he would do when the time came. All he knew was that defending

Kathryn and the Kirsch children was the priority right now. Whatever had to be done would be...a mission was never abandoned before completion.

CHAPTER 7

The nearly twelve hour ride from Kentucky to DC was uneventful, not counting the 20 or so minutes Kathryn and Rube spent bickering about music. They settled on some CDs Jules made for the trip…songs they didn't always recognize but could live with. Paul was wrapped in a blanket sound asleep in the back seat. He never woke up.

Kathryn checked on him occasionally, particularly the two times they stopped for gas, food, and rest. Wherever he'd been, they deprived him of sleep as well as blood. It was almost 9am Sunday morning when the Suburban pulled up the driveway of the Kirsch manor. Dev came in behind Rube in his black van; the spirits brought up the rear on Harleys.

"I'll help you." Rube said, getting out of the driver's seat.

"No, I can do it." Kathryn picked Paul up in her arms, still wrapped in the blanket to protect him from the sunlight, and walked up onto the porch.

"Mother," Nathan stood in the shadows so the sunlight wouldn't touch him. "Is he alright?"

"Yes, love. Come upstairs with me."

They moved past Rube and up the stairs to Paul's large bedroom. Charlie and Halle rushed in behind them. Kathryn laid Paul on the bed. He opened his eyes, taking in his surroundings.

"Deti[vii]," He whispered, reaching out for them. "My little spitfire. I've missed you so; I love you so. Plot ot ploti. Krov ot krovi."

"I missed you, Daddy." Halle kissed his face. "We were so afraid that you would never come back to us."

"Father," Nathan managed a smile when Paul lovingly slapped his cheek. "I never gave up hope. I love you."

"I love you too, my son. Charlie…"

"It's so good to see you," Charlie said. "I did everything I could to help them find you."

"I know you did." Paul replied.

"He's very weak," Kathryn told them. "He needs to feed."

"I'll help." Charlie rolled up his sleeve.

"So will I, Mother."

"You can't, Nath," Kathryn caressed his face.

"Why not? I want to help."

"I know you do but you were so sick when you were born. We have to be careful right now; I know you understand." She kissed his forehead and glanced at Halle. "You need to do this."

Halle gave a solemn nod and held out her wrist. She would do anything for her father, even deal with the pain of a feed. He'd done that and much more for her over the centuries.

"My beloved little warrior." Paul kissed the inside of her wrist before clamping down on it with his fangs.

He didn't take too much, just as he hadn't from Kathryn. Charlie made him take more from him to make up for it. Paul needed it right now and the younger vampires were healthy and strong. Paul was reluctant but Charlie was insistent. So he did, feeling more like himself when the feeding was through. Kathryn went about making sure they were both tightly bandaged. Luckily puncture holes wouldn't bleed too much, even when connected to major arteries.

Johanna burst into the door as they were cleaning up. *Thank God*, Kathryn thought to herself, her little one had never seen a feeding. They were only drinking by the time she was born almost 75 years ago. She ran straight for the bed, not caring about anything else happening in the room.

"Daddy!" She exclaimed.

"Mein kleiner schatz[viii]." Paul opened his arms for her.

"Daddy, Daddy!" Johanna jumped into bed and into his embrace. Paul held her tight, kissing her forehead.

"Where were you, Daddy? I missed you so much. Nath said you were bringing me presents…what did you bring me?"

"Calm down, sweetheart." Kathryn stroked her fingers through the mass of brown curls on her head. "Daddy fell ill while he was away; he'll need to rest for a few days."

"I'll help you rest, Daddy." Johanna hugged him tighter. "I promise."

"I know you will, leibling[ix]." Paul kissed her face.

Kathryn smiled at the sight of him surrounded by their family. She wasn't sure if she would ever see it again. While she didn't know what would happen next, she pushed that feeling aside for just a few moments to enjoy her family's happiness. She wouldn't let anyone take that away from her.

Standing up from the bed, Kathryn left the bedroom. She walked down the long hallway, the stairs, and into the library. Rube, Dev, the spirits, Jules, and Bash were in various states of relaxation. Despite the scene, the gnawing sense of danger was still in Kathryn's stomach. It was stronger than ever standing in that room.

"Jules," She asked. "Is this over?"

"There is always more to endure." The augur replied. "You know that."

"This isn't over," Falconer said, looking out the picture window onto a manicured lawn. "I feel the scavengers close."

"Well I can't just have you guys stick to me like glue in anticipation of an attack that may never come." Kathryn said. "Paul should be OK in a few days."

"Surely this Marin will strike when he thinks you're most defenseless." Rube said. He sat on the edge of the couch going over in his head how he would fight a menace completely unknown to him.

"We'll stick around for a few days." Sam added, looking at Falconer. The Apache nodded. "What are your plans, Dev?" Sam asked.

"It's not a proper mission until I get to kick a little ass." Dev replied. "I'm in. Rubidoux?"

"I'm not going anywhere."

Kathryn looked at him when he said it. He meant it. She wondered if it was for any other reason than his life was in danger now too. She wasn't sure how to ask. She wasn't sure of anything anymore concerning Special Agent Alexander Rubidoux.

"I don't know how to thank all of you." She said. "Just when I forget there is goodness even in our world…"

"You know how to thank me," Dev replied. "No more freebies, your highness."

"Cross my heart."

"Well, we should get going." Jules said. She took Kathryn's hand. "There is more work to be done today."

"Of course. I will never be able to repay you for all you've done. Looking after my children…"

"I was happy to do it." Jules replied. "They're a rowdy crew but good kids."

"There is a way to repay." Bash said. At six foot one, she towered over Kathryn. But there was nothing frightening about her presence. She brought as much calm as Jules did. "Continue to walk as close to the light as you can. Despite your affliction, don't let the darkness embrace your essence." She took her other hand and squeezed.

"I promise."

Kathryn was about to walk them to the door when the library doors flew open.

"Surprise." Marin grinned. It didn't take long for it to turn into a sneer. "Don't tell me you're not happy to see me. I'm so happy to see you, Ekaterina; it's been ages. How are the children?"

At his side as always was his mate, Lex. Behind them stood the remainder of their clan, Raphael Black and Nicholas Grafton. Julian, Raphael's son, used to walk with them as well. Paul killed him in self-defense 92 years ago in a dark Petrograd alley. Dev and the spirits drew their weapons as the Reapers came for them. Rube knew his gun would be useless in this battle. The immortal threw him a pipe the size of a baseball bat with a bend on the end allowing him to jump into the melee as well. Kathryn grabbed Bash and Jules, who grabbed Morian, and smuggled them behind the secret wall.

"These stairs will take you directly to a wall that leads into Paul's room." She whispered. "Hurry, he and the children are there alone. We'll keep their hands full down here."

They nodded, rushing up the steep stairs with the Rottweiler in tow. Kathryn ran down a narrow hallway, pushing another wall that brought her into the dining room. She reached up for the sword on the wall. Paul always told the children he used that sword to survive The Crusades. Kathryn hoped it was as helpful today as she ran back to the library. Lex immediately went at her with a stake.

"Die bitch!" Lex exclaimed.

"You first," Kathryn knocked the stake out of her hand. The sword was heavy, not easy for her to wield. She'd had her share of sword fights over the years but it'd been a while. Kath had to plant her feet; get the job done. No one she loved would die today.

It didn't take long for Mandy to get Grafton on the ground. He was lazy and out of shape. Spirits weren't supposed to express hate or anger. Still, they'd been human once and those emotions could sometimes be difficult to suppress. Mandy hated him as much as she allowed herself to hate someone. 20 odd years ago Nicholas went rogue, even for a Reaper, and committed a series of grisly coed murders in Nebraska. 10 women were killed and authorities never solved the case.

The Council, including Paul Kirsch, was so disgusted by his actions that they forced The Darkness to suspend his reaping activities for a decade and confine him to darkest pit of The Barrens. When his sentence was up, he went right back to his clan. Mandy didn't think that was enough for the pain he'd caused. Having him on his knees, she knew he was finally going to get the punishment he deserved.

She took the sword Falconer threw to her and cut the Reaper's head off. He let out an agonizing cry before turning into a puddle of tar-like goo on the carpet. Mandy rushed into the fight Jacob and Dev were having with Raphael. He was not going to be as easy.

Marin was a wily adversary for Sam and Rube. He was almost a thousand years old, one of the oldest and most feared Reapers still roaming the Earth. His speed and agility were the envy of those around him. Rube went for his knees with the pipe but Marin kicked it out of his hands. Then he kicked Rube in the face. Rube went down, only for a moment, but it was enough time for Marin to run from the library.

"Split up," Sam said. "I'll take the back and you take the front."

Rube nodded. He didn't want to leave Kathryn but with Marin possibly on the upper levels of the house, no one was safe. He picked the pipe up from the floor, breaking into a run. Rube's heart beat so quickly, just like the night he chased that lightning bug. His eyes darted all around as he made his way through the darkened living room, up the stairs, and into the hallway. It looked deserted but he knew looks could be deceiving.

000

Raphael picked up one of the antique chairs, smashing it over Dev's back. As Dev fell, he raised his scythe to take the immortal's head. He was sneering, thinking about how lovely it would look on his wall. Mandy unleashed a barrage of Chinese stars on his unprotected chest and torso, making him fall forward. The black ooze that passed for Reaper blood spilled everywhere. He'd hardly hit the floor before Falconer took his head. There was another screech of pain as Raphael turned into a puddle of black goo. Mandy reached a hand out to help Dev from the floor.

"I owe you one." He said.

"Spirits don't collect markers." She replied.

"We may have to reconsider that." Falconer said.

Kathryn flew into them. Lex was on the war path and she didn't plan on stopping until they were all dead. She took quite a lot of joy from her job. The scythe only had one more dedicated to it...he was now closer to the Kirsch family than anyone wanted him to be. Lex could feel him, got her strength from him, and it was time to end this.

"You're all going to die, and I'm going to enjoy every moment of it." She said, swinging her scythe with precision. "Who wants to be first?"

"I really don't like her." Dev said, planting his feet into the carpet for another battle. It was four against one and they would take her out.

000

Rube stood in the middle of the hallway, not sure which way to go first. There were six doors that opened into large rooms. There was also a bathroom. Marin could be hiding anywhere. If he had to search them all, he would, but it would take time. The Reaper flew by, crashing hard into him. Rube hit the wall and cursed.

"Show yourself, you bastard! Fight like a man."

He could hear Marin's laughter echoing off every wall. Rube would never be able to tell which direction it was coming from. It surrounded him like something out of a horror movie.

"Rube!"

He turned when he heard Sam at the top of the back stairs.

"You take the front three and I'll handle the back three. We're going to find him."

The FBI agent nodded, doing his best to shake off the stars in his head. It was a hard hit but it would take more than that to knock him out. He opened Nathan's bedroom door and stepped in.

000

Kathryn didn't want to admit the joy she got finally stabbing Lex in the chest. It hardly seemed to affect her, though she was bleeding profusely. Dev kicked her legs out from under her and she fell. Lex was tired. It had been a hard fight, four against one, and she held on as long as she could. Reapers weren't used to long, arduous battles…they preferred the element of surprise. One rarely fought hard when you crept into their homes and slaughtered them in their sleep. Finally on her knees, she spit black goo onto the carpet.

"Do whatever you have to, you bloodsucking bitch." She said. "I would if I were you. Believe me."

"I do." Kathryn replied, swiftly decapitating her.

Lex screamed before a heavy silence fell over the room. It was just a few moments later that they heard another agonizing howl. Beaten, battered, and exhausted, the four of them rushed for the stairs.

000

Rube heard the scream come from the master bedroom; Kathryn's room. He ran toward it and kicked the door open. Kathryn was lying on the floor completely covered in blood.

"No! Kath!" Rube rushed to her, picking up her lifeless body in his arms. "Oh God, Kathryn." He held her close and rocked her gently. "What happened to you?"

Her hand reached up for his face and Rube felt a glimmer of hope. There were only three ways to kill a vampire. She still had her head and there were no stakes in her heart. She lost a lot of blood but maybe there was still a chance. Kathryn snatched the amulet from his neck with a wicked grin.

"Kath…" Rube gasped when he felt a long blade enter his side.

All five of them, Kathryn, Sam, Dev, Mandy, and Falconer rushed into the room as he dropped the no longer lifeless body.

"Alexander!" she exclaimed.

He tried to turn, immediately recognized her voice. Instead he watched in horror while the bloody Kathryn in front of him morphed into Michael Marin.

"No hard feelings, cowboy, right?" The Reaper asked grinning. "I hope it hurts terribly. It looks as if it does."

Rube tried to get on his feet but stumbled and fell to his knees. Kathryn rushed to catch him as everyone else jumped on Marin. She pulled him back toward the chest of drawers, out of harm's way. Rube lay in her arms, struggling to catch his breath as blood filled his lungs. Kathryn went to pull out the knife but he took her hand away.

"Don't do that, I'll die if you do that."

"Oh God, Alexander."

"I thought it was you." His voice was hardly a whisper. "I thought he hurt you; I couldn't bear it."

"The bastard can shape shift. I didn't tell you…this is my fault."

"I'm sorry, Kath."

"Don't you dare apologize. Just don't die on me now. Please, Alexander."

"The other side awaits us all." He quoted Jules. "With open arms." He coughed, blood coming out of his mouth. He felt cold but there was warmth someplace close. He needed to get to it; feel it in his bones.

"You can stay here, just say the word. Tell me that you want to stay with me."

"If you bite me I will never forgive you. I couldn't bear to hate you for eternity, don't you make me. I'm sorry I can't take you to dinner. I think we both deserved a night off. I was looking forward to it more than I should have. Looking forward to being with you."

"Don't die on me, Alex." Kathryn held him tighter. "I just…please don't go yet. Please don't go."

"I don't want you to be sad." Rube grimaced in pain. "You have to let go; I can see the light."

"Absolutely not," Tears streamed down her face. "I need you to stay with me. Just stay with me."

"It's almost over." Rube whispered. "Kathryn, I…"

His body went limp in her arms, blue eyes still staring up at her. Kathryn cried out just as Mandy flew into the chest of drawers beside them. Toiletries fell down like rain but neither woman paid it much mind.

"He's trying to get away!" The blonde exclaimed, getting up and shaking off the pain.

Marin jumped onto the window seat. He went to kick out the glass but Sam's arrow pierced his shoulder. The Reaper grimaced, spinning around, another arrow quickly hitting his chest and then his leg. He started to fall backward. Dev yanked him forward, kept him from falling out of the window. If he got out there then he was as good as gone. He snatched the amulet out of Marin's hand and threw him to his knees.

"Get ready to join your harlot in hell." Dev said, unable to hold back his anger.

Falconer handed Sam his sword. Sam took a deep breath, knowing the beheading had to take place but couldn't come from a place of vengeance. He was only a human but he had to fight the darkness.

"This is for New Jersey," Sam said. "And Alexander Rubidoux."

He took Marin's head in one swoop, the body falling over on the carpet. As it turned to goo, Mandy opened the window and scattered the liquid into the atmosphere with a flick of her wrist. No one had ever come back from decapitation but she'd make damn sure Michael Marin was the first to defy the odds. There were other Reapers to take his place; surely another problem for another day.

The sudden quiet was pierced by Kathryn's sobbing. They all looked at her, sitting on the floor. She was surrounded by a puddle of darkening blood and held Rube's dead body in her arms.

"We need to take him now." Sam said, gently approaching her.

"Stay away from him!" Kathryn shouted.

"He's gone, Kath. His soul needs to be at peace."

"He wouldn't let me bring him over, Sam. I was willing to but he said he wouldn't forgive me. He didn't want to be with me."

"That's not his destiny." Mandy replied.

"Kathryn, please, we have to…"

"Don't touch him, Sam." Her eyes turned black as her fangs slid out of her gums.

Sam took a step back though he knew Kathryn wouldn't hurt him. Mandy brushed past him, crouching down beside the grieving woman.

"He died protecting you and your children." Mandy said in a soothing tone, her hand on Kathryn's shoulder. "Let me take him to the light he so richly deserves."

"Will he be content there?" Kathryn asked. She was still clutching his hand to her heart, their fingers intertwined.

"There is nothing but love and serenity in the light. Rube deserves it; will be surrounded by it for eternity."

Kathryn nodded. Mandy was finally able to coax the dead man from her arms. She picked him up, moving into the middle of the floor. Enormous, silver-white wings came from her shoulder blades. Mandy disappeared in a glowing white light and Sam comforted Kathryn. Spirits were able to bring calm to chaos...soon she was composed enough to stand.

"The Reapers are dead," Falconer said. "Our job is done and we have to move on."

"Thank you." Kathryn squeezed his hand. She hugged Sam tight, hardly wanting to let him go. She lost Rube and now the spirit would leave her behind as well.

"I am never far away when you need me, Kath." He whispered in her ear. "Just call my name. Yell it if you have to. I'll always hear you."

He pulled out of her embrace. He smacked his fist against Dev's, Falconer did the same, and they walked out of the room. Kathryn watched them walk down the hall and then the stairs. She heard them leave the house, listened to the roar of their motorcycles as they rode away.

It was over. Just like that everything was over. Kathryn's whole life took eleven days to change and less than an hour to return to "normal". Dev put his hand on her shoulder. Kathryn looked at him.

"You need to be with your family now." He said. "They're probably worried about you."

"I can't let them see me like this. I'm covered in blood, Dev."

"Well get cleaned up. I'm going to call a guy I trust; he'll send a team to clean up the rest of this mess." He couldn't help but look at Rube's blood soaking the crème carpet. Dammit. "I'll leave you alone for a while."

"Thank you. Can you please check on my family? Let them know that I'm safe but please don't tell them about Alexander."

Dev nodded, walking out of the room and closing the door behind him. Kathryn stood in that same spot for a long while and closed her eyes. She didn't know who to talk to, what to ask for, so she just thought of him. She thought of his strength, his tenacity, and his dimple. She thought of how he looked at her the first night they met.

She thought of how he looked at her on the way home from Kentucky. She thought of him calling her a good mother and helping her nurse her wound after the lightning bug attack. The world deserved Alexander Rubidoux…it wouldn't be as bright without him. Walking over to the window, Kathryn looked out on an increasingly cloudy day.

"Please take care of him, Sam." She said, pressing her hand on the glass.

CHAPTER 8

Kathryn sat at her vanity table six weeks later, brushing her long, raven hair. Evanescence was on her CD player; she'd been listening to the same song on repeat for hours. The tears had come and gone for what might as well have been the thousandth time. She had given up trying to stop them. It was better to admit her powerlessness and let them have their moment. Paul knocked on the door before coming in.

"Is she asleep?" Kathryn asked. She tried to smile but fell short. She'd been falling short for a while now. No one called her on it, not even Johanna who called her mother on everything. A pall had fallen over the entire house.

"Soundly, though she insisted on two chapters of *Alice of Wonderland* tonight."

"Insisted? She is eight years old Paul, and you are an overindulgent father."

"She was so adorable when she asked." He replied. "She's my sweet little leibling. If a father can't overindulge his children then the world isn't worth living in."

"Johanna has you eating out of her hands. They all do, you know. Paul, I have to say this will be the last birthday party for me."

"You said that last year, luybov."

"Well I really mean it this time. I'm tired of hyperactive children, noise, games, and clowns. I fuckin hate clowns." Kathryn shuddered. "Johanna can't even eat birthday cake, Nathan has a sweet tooth so he eats until he's nauseous, and I hate clowns."

"You mentioned that, Katya." Paul laughed gently. He put his hands on her shoulders, fingers massaging her skin.

"Where are the children?" She asked, her body stiffening at his touch. Kathryn didn't want this. She didn't want it and her stomach turned at the idea that that might not matter.

"Halle and Nathan went out for the evening."

"Together?"

"Of course not; Nathan said he was heading to the library. Charlie is downstairs playing chess. I'll probably join him in a little while. However…"

He pulled her up from the chair, wrapping her in his embrace. Kathryn let him kiss her but held him off when he slid down the strap of her nightgown.

"Katya…"

"I don't want to make love." She walked toward the window. "I don't want you touching me. I can't, Paul. I'm sorry."

"You haven't let me touch you since I returned." He said. "What's the matter with you?"

"We were having troubles before you were taken. Those things don't just disappear. That you thought they would…that's so you, Paul. I can't do this anymore."

"Don't you know how much I love you?"

"It would be insulting for me to say that you don't love me and I don't want to do that." Kathryn said. She also wasn't in the mood for a fight. "You love me in the way that you know how. That way has never been enough. I feel the need to apologize for that, but I can't apologize for what isn't my fault. It's not me, it's you Paul. But I've stood by your side for over 500 years so I'll take my part of the blame."

"Not every moment." Paul replied.

"Every time I left I was seeking something that I couldn't find. All these years later and I hardly know what it was. Still, there's a void in me that this can no longer fill. I've probably known that for longer than I care to admit. Saying it aloud is the most painful thing I've ever had to do." Kathryn clutched her chest. For the first time in six weeks, her heart was aching for a reason that wasn't Alexander Rubidoux. "I need to be fulfilled...I'm practically empty."

"You're leaving me?"

"I have nowhere to go." She said.

"That's not an answer, Katya."

He wanted to reach out but she was so far away. Paul would be lying to himself if he said Kathryn hadn't been far away for a long time. A part of him knew that she would never leave him. Kathryn had some of her own money, she was certainly talented enough to make more. But Paul always convinced her to stay. He told her that she and the children would have difficulties without him. He could keep them safe; he would always love and care for them. It wasn't always perfect but he was meant to lead them. They were blood of my blood...without Paul, they were nothing.

"I'm sorry that he's dead; I'm so sorry." Paul said. He wasn't sorry but it was the right thing to say.

"What are you talking about?"

Kathryn couldn't look at him; she stared out the window instead. There was a beautiful purple sky and silver half-moon. She felt as if she didn't deserve to see such magnificence. She couldn't help but wonder what Alexander would think of it.

"I'm talking about Alexander Rubidoux from the FBI. He's the one in your heart. Please don't lie to me...I can feel you. I can feel your anguish."

"You're alive because Alexander risked his life for this family. He sacrificed everything for someone he didn't even know. He said it was his job but it was more than that. This world perplexed him but he never…he was a courageous man, Paul."

"And you gave him your heart." Paul replied, walking over to the window and standing beside her. "What else did you give to him? Your love for him is a force of its own. How did you think you could hide something like this from me? Our blood runs through each other's veins, Katya. I will always know your heart and mind."

"It doesn't matter…Alexander is dead." She said.

"But it matters to me."

"I don't care. I'm not going to discuss him with you." Kathryn's tone was angry, defensive, but she had tears in her eyes. "He isn't yours to share."

"You don't have to say a word. You're with me because you can't be with him." Paul tempered his anger. His stomach felt sick. Never, never had he ever felt what he felt emanating from Kathryn; never once in over 500 years. There had been other men, most of whom he quickly did away with.

This was something else altogether. That bastard was lucky he was already dead. Of course maybe if he wasn't whatever they had would've fizzled out. Now Alexander Rubidoux got to be Kathryn's forever hero. "I feel him deep inside of you, this goddamn human I don't even know. I never imagined another soul could be so deep inside of you. How could you?"

"You have no right to ask me that and you know it. I'm here with you because you are my family. Plot ot ploti, krov ot krovi, always. I've been devoted to making this work for centuries despite knowing that it wasn't. Allow me time to grieve, for whatever its worth."

"Maybe one day," Paul slipped one arm around her waist, brushed her hair aside, and nipped the nape of her neck. He wanted to possess her again but she moved from his embrace. "We might find our way back to each other. I will never stop loving you." even as he said it, he knew that would never be the case. Paul knew Kathryn better than she knew herself most of the time; she was gone. She might stay in his home, might even return to his bed, but she was gone.

"There is likely much life left for me to live. That is my curse."

"I've always thought of it as a blessing, Katya. I thought you did as well."

She didn't respond so Paul stroked her hair and wished her goodnight. He left her alone. Kathryn didn't want to think anymore…she was tired of thinking. She closed the bedroom door, turned out the lights, and slid into bed. She made a sound of anguish as she wiped the feeling of his lips from her skin. Her dreams were the only place she felt peace. How much longer she could live like this, Kathryn wasn't sure. She wanted to be released from the constant torture.

"Help me," She whispered. "Someone please help me."

***

DC was finally cool, nearing cold but Connelly's office was stuffy. Kathryn sat on the plush couch, legs crossed, and waited for him. She'd been waiting over a half hour but Kathryn was blessed with patience many years ago. She didn't need to leaf through year old magazines, excessively check her watch or tap her foot, he would be there. He walked in exactly on time and smiled.

"Hello there." He said. "Damn, you look amazing."

"Really? I just threw this on." She replied, standing.

"I would love to watch that process."

Kathryn wore a red business dress, red high heels, and a black hat with a wide brim tied with a red scarf. Connelly took a moment to drink her in; she was a whole lot of woman. He sat behind his desk and offered her a cigarette.

"I thought smoking was illegal in federal buildings, Senator."

"Lots of things are illegal. We do them anyway…we love the adrenaline rush."

"Tell me about it." Kathryn sat in the chair, slipping the cigarette between her red lips. Connelly lit it.

"How is Paul? I've been trying to nail him down for dinner; he is quite a busy man. It's nearly impossible."

"He's in Barcelona right now on business. He's fully recovered and back to doing what he does best."

"And the children?" Connelly asked.

"Stef, did you set Paul up?" Kathryn countered with a question of her own.

"Absolutely not. I may be privy to certain government projects, The Council is as well. Paul is a member of The Council. I would never do something like that to him. He's been quite helpful to me over the years…that's not how one repays a friend."

"He isn't your friend."

"Speaking of friends, Alexander Rubidoux has taken an indefinite leave of absence from the FBI." Stephen said. "Do you know anything about that?"

"No," Kathryn shook her head. Her stomach dropped just hearing his name. It took all the strength Kathryn possessed, and that was a lot, to keep her neutral face. She deeply inhaled the cigarette. It was expensive, foreign, and flavorful. She would focus on it instead of how hearing someone else say Alex's name made her feel.

"I don't think he's taken as much as a sick day nearly 20 years in the Bureau. Now he requests a leave of absence in a letter."

"He obviously had plenty of time stored up." She replied. Kathryn had no idea who wrote that letter for Rube but it was probably better that way. She didn't need to be involved in that anymore; she'd been through enough.

"Where is he, Kathryn?"

"Why do you think I would have the answer to that? He did his job for me and that was it. You're the watcher, not me. You're Agent Rubidoux's friend, not me. I'm sure you have some unnamed source dying to tell you all about it, Senator. Go and pick on them."

Kathryn focused on her cigarette, shutting off pieces of her consciousness. The most important thing to her was to relax. Losing it in front of Connelly was not an option. She smiled though her stomach was churning and she felt nauseous. That wasn't a feeling she was used to and it was difficult to conceal.

"I heard it was a hard battle." He changed the subject. "Your home was the scene of much carnage."

"We won, those bastard reapers are dead…that's all that matters to me. Alexander kept my family safe and I won't concern myself with anything else."

"So revenge isn't on your list of things to do before years end?" Connelly asked. "It isn't on Paul's?"

"I thought Paul was your friend; you don't know his deepest thoughts? I'm done with the entire thing. I'm sure, despite what people think that it would be easy to locate and kill Karen Pierson. In the end that makes me no better than whoever she is. Just know this, and tell it to whomever you tell things to, if anyone else comes near my family again, I'm taking heads. I'm taking them, putting them on sticks and parading them on the steps of the Capitol. This is not a test Senator, it's a promise." Kathryn put the cigarette out on the desk and watched Connelly grimace. She stood, smoothing out her dress.

"I'll let it be known." Connelly replied. "It's always lovely to see you, Kathryn."

"Let's make sure we don't have to do this for some time to come."

"If you like it then I love it." Stephen smiled. "Please send Paul my regards."

"Good afternoon, Senator." Kathryn walked out of his office and to the elevator. She touched her big red purse; it was holding the gun Connelly gave Alex years ago. She had planned to give it back to him today but didn't have the heart. The idea of having to see him again wasn't overly pleasant.

Still, Kathryn knew he deserved to have his piece of Alex, probably even more so than she did. Connelly would know the whole story soon enough…Watchers found out everything. Maybe he already knew and just wanted to hear it from her. Kathryn hoped he wasn't holding his breath. Actually, she hoped that he was.

***

Dusk was her favorite part of the day. Late November meant much colder nights but that never bothered her. Kathryn sat on a park bench, watching the world go by. She sipped blood from a Starbucks cup and sighed. A pink rose appeared in front of her and she smiled. Turning around, she saw Sam; Kathryn leaned to kiss his lips. He came around to sit beside her.

"How are you?" He asked.

Kathryn shrugged, sipping her drink. She took a deep breath and let the wave of sadness pass. It had been nine weeks since Alexander died in her arms. Kathryn was still struggling to move on. The tears had mostly dried but she found her feet still planted in the same spot. She didn't have the heart to walk away because it was like walking away from him.

"You can talk to me." Sam's voice was soft and comforting. He put his hand over hers in her lap.

"I'm getting by, Sam. Some days I'm fine, and then I'm not so fine. Then I cry more than I ever have in my life. I cry until there is nothing left. Then I smile, before this blinding numbness falls over me. That's usually followed by anger and more tears. Is that what you wanted to know?"

"There are seven stages of grief." He replied.

"I know that, and I've experienced them all about three times. When will this dreadful pain subside, Sam?"

"Soon, I would say."

"How do you know?" Kathryn asked.

"What do you mean how do I know? I have super, secret, and special powers; that's how. That's a true statement. You of all people should know that."

Kathryn smiled at him. Sam took a hold of her hand.

"You've always wondered how I found you." He asked. "In Warsaw."

"Yes. There aren't many unanswered questions in my life, but that one…"

"You prayed for me."

"What?"

"You prayed for me, Kathryn."

"I absolutely did not." She smirked, shaking her head. "I don't think I've ever prayed in my life. I don't even know how to pray."

"You were pretty bad at it." Sam replied with a soft smile. "It wasn't much; you just said 'Please help us. If anyone out there can hear me, I need help'."

"Oh my God." She really looked at him. "I remember that. I remember what I felt when I said it."

"The Boss heard you and he sent me. The Boss always hears your prayers, Kath, no matter how lousy they sound to you."

"Are you serious? Sam, that's…are you serious? How am I supposed to handle that?"

"It's usually a little heavy for first timers. Just take some time to let it sink in and tell me how your family is."

"Paul is back to doing what he always does. He works hard and forgets all the promises he made to be there. Some things never change. Luckily I stopped believing him a long time ago. Jules Sohn is going to help Charlie get a job with the FBI. He needs to put all of his knowledge to good use and I think he'll be happy there. It's so important that Paul no longer be our only lifeline to the outside world.

"Halle has met a man. Oh God, I'm so worried. He is good to her; they've been together about six weeks. He's older, mature, and not a vampire. I'm the one who told her to stay away from vampires. Since they've started dating she has shown a maturity I wasn't sure she was capable of. That doesn't mean I don't lie awake at night, waiting for the phone call that she's set fire to his house or murdered his parakeets in some kind of impetuous rage."

"You're experiencing what every mother does." Sam replied. "Your baby may leave the nest soon."

"You're going to freak me out Sam," Kathryn looked at him. "Stop it."

"Tell me about Nath." Sam smiled.

"He wants to learn to bartend and maybe do some cooking. He's been hanging out at Absinthe...Max Ryan has taken him under his wing. Nath shows a propensity for it and is learning the ropes quickly. He's content right now. I love my son more than anything but I don't think I've ever seen him experience such contentment. It's been almost 20 months since his last blood lust incident.

"I can't pretend it won't happen again but if his mind remains occupied with other things then there is a better chance, you know? Johanna is busy with her swim lessons, Schopenhauer readings, and learning Brahms on the piano. It's been a long time, Sam, but I think we're finally coming out of the exile Paul imposed on the family when we came to DC. I know that I'm tired of living behind heavy curtains. I have to break free even if I have no idea what lies ahead for me."

"It'll come to you, I promise." Sam replied. "You are a formidable woman."

"Thank you." She squeezed his hand. "I need to thank you for everything. I'm still here because of you. You saved me and my children...twice. There is nothing I can do to repay you."

"I brought a birthday gift for the little one." He pulled the pink box from his jacket pocket.

"Sam, she's already spoiled enough." Kathryn took the box. "Believe me."

"What kind of guardian angel forgets his favorite charge's birthday? Open it, do you think Johanna will like it."

Kathryn pulled the top from the box and moved the tissue paper. It was a silver and amethyst angel pendant on a sterling silver chain. The little note inside said, '*I'm always close when you need me. Love, Guardian Angel Sam*'.

"Oh Sam, it's beautiful. Johanna's going to adore it…she really is. I'm sorry you won't be able to give it to her yourself."

"She does give the best hugs but I won't be in town long enough. I have a gift for you too though, before I go."

"A gift for me? You really didn't have to do that. You've given me so much already."

"This is important. It's one of the reasons I came to see you tonight." Sam said. "Turn around."

"What?" She raised an eyebrow.

"Turn around."

"Why?" she smiled. "Have you hidden my gift in the bushes?"

"Turn around, Kath."

The sound of another voice made her freeze. She looked at Sam with wide brown eyes. Opening her mouth to speak, Kathryn sputtered over the words.

"Oh my God, Sam…Sam…oh my…"

Kathryn turned around and saw Rube. She let out a whimper of joy, jumping up and rushing into his arms. He held her tight to him, exhaling. Sam stood from the bench and walked away. They needed a moment alone.

"I can't believe it's you." She said. "Oh my God, this is…I've missed you so much." She broke down in tears.

"I've missed you too." Rube whispered against her raven hair. He rubbed her back, the sound of her anguish so difficult to hear. In his arms she slowly found comfort.

"Is it really you?" Kathryn caressed his face, stroked the skin. He felt real. Nothing ever felt more real. "I watched you die...you can't be here now. You died in my arms; I can't stop replaying it over and over in my head. I begged you to stay but you refused."

"Well I'm here now, in your arms."

"How?"

"I'm walking in the light, Kathryn."

Recognition immediately dawned on her face, which broke out in a smile.

"Of course you are; so few souls shine brighter. Alexander, I've thought of you every moment of everyday. I could hardly focus on anything else. I thought I was going to lose my mind without you. There were so many things I wanted to say but it was too late. I couldn't live with it being too late."

"Ditto. You weren't as beautiful in my thoughts as you are in my arms, Kathryn. And you never left my thoughts."

She smiled, kissing him for the first time. It was deep, passionate, and filled her with indescribable joy. Kathryn knew she only felt something similar once before, the first time she kissed Paul half a millennia ago. It made her feel dizzy and giddy. With Paul, it could've been a trick. With Alexander, nothing was more real.

"I still owe you dinner." Rube said, his lips over hers. His fingers traced her warm cheeks and he closed his eyes. "My God, you are so warm."

"So are you." Kathryn quivered from the contact, which was nearly orgasmic. She was breathing in short, excited spurts. "Your essence is amazing. Alexander, oh Alexander." She kept whispering his name as she tried to hold his body. How was such love and warmth even possible? "How long can you stay with me?"

"I'll only be in town for few days." Rube replied. "I have to formally resign from the FBI. Then there are a few more loose ends to wrap up before heading off to Belgrade for a little bit."

"You'll be with Sam?"

"Yeah, he's my guardian for the time being. I get along well with the team. Though spirit teams are usually threesomes, The Boss thinks four is good for us."

"You'll be unstoppable." Kathryn said, kissing him again. "Still, you just got back; I don't want you to leave so soon. I need to hold you. Don't leave me again."

"You know that I must, but not before our Friday night dinner reservation at Charlie Palmer's. We have a lot to talk about."

"I love steak."

"I know," Rube never wanted to stop kissing her. She felt so good in his arms, close to him. Being able to feel her essence was so amazing that words would never properly describe it. "Kath, I don't know how or when but my feelings for you run so deep…straight to my very soul. Even in the light, being without you was difficult. I kept thinking about your Jedi analogy to spirits."

"Yes, but I also said love is the strongest of all emotions."

"It won't be easy…I'll be gone a lot. The separation might be agonizing for the both of us."

"I will always be here when you return." Kathryn replied. "You'll always have a home here."

"So you'll wait for me?" He asked.

"Forever; longer than that. I promise you. I love you and I'll never stop."

"There are rules, Kath." It was hard but Rube put a bit of distance between them. He still held her in his arms; he couldn't do anything but. "I shouldn't even have kissed you but I couldn't help myself. As long as your heart and soul belong to another, we cannot be together. I'm not telling you that to force your hand, please believe me. Your bond with Paul is strong…you have a family and a history. I only want you to follow your heart, even if it leads you away from me."

Rube hugged her close again. He didn't want to let her go but his life was different now. With all he was about to embark on, Rube couldn't be in the middle of a love triangle as well. He was risking enough just feeling and expressing what was in his heart. He couldn't help that. But infidelity was a mortal sin. He couldn't have the wife of another in his bed and walk in the light. It didn't work that way.

"Feel my heart," Kathryn took his hand and put it over her silver patch. "It belongs to you and no other. I'd give you my soul if I had one. I've lived one life for over 500 years…I want something else now. I want you, Alexander Rubidoux."

"I want you too. I'll take your heart and carry it with me, I promise. I have to go now. We'll see each other on Friday."

"I'm counting the moments." She said. "Tell me you're doing the same."

"I am. I have been since the last time I left your arms. It's the last tragedy I ever want us to endure."

Rube kissed her once more and they parted. He walked across the park to where Sam stood. Sam waved at Kathryn, holding his other hand over his heart. She blew him a kiss and did the same. Sam caught the kiss before the two men turned and walked away. Kathryn headed home in the other direction. She looked up at the night sky. It wasn't often that the stars shone so brightly in the city but tonight they were spectacular.

"Thank you," She whispered. "I don't know what to believe but I believe in my feelings for Alexander Rubidoux. I owe you everything for bringing him back to me. No matter how long it takes, I plan to repay. I have all the time in the world to do it."

<u>NOTES</u>

---

[i] love

[ii] my

[iii] Flesh of my flesh

[iv] Blood of my blood

[v] forever

[vi] Paul

[vii] daughter

[viii] My little sweetheart

[ix] darling

Made in the USA
Columbia, SC
06 October 2017